EMPTY
SET

EMPTY SET

ø

Verónica Gerber Bicecci

Translated by Christina MacSweeney

COFFEE HOUSE PRESS

Minneapolis | 2018

First English-language edition published 2018
Copyright © 2015 by Verónica Gerber Bicecci,
c/o Indent Literary Agency, www.indentagency.com
Translation © 2018 by Christina MacSweeney
Cover design by Kyle G. Hunter

Originally published by Almadía Ediciones as *Conjunto vacío,* © 2015

Coffee House Press books are available to the trade through our pri-
mary distributor, Consortium Book Sales & Distribution, cbsd.com
or (800) 283–3572. For personal orders, catalogs, or other information,
write to info@coffeehousepress.org.

Coffee House Press is a nonprofit literary publishing house. Support
from private foundations, corporate giving programs, government
programs, and generous individuals helps make the publication of
our books possible. We gratefully acknowledge their support in detail
in the back of this book.

LIBRARY OF CONGRESS CATALOGING-IN-PUBLICATION DATA
Names: Gerber Bicecci, Verónica, 1981- author. | MacSweeney,
    Christina, translator.
Title: Empty set / Verónica Gerber Bicecci ; translated by
    Christina MacSweeney.
Other titles: Conjunto vacío. English
Description: Minneapolis : Coffee House Press, 2018. | Translated
    from Spanish.
Identifiers: LCCN 2017030786 | ISBN 9781566894944 (paperback)
Subjects: LCSH: Families—Fiction. | Loss (Psychology)—Fiction. |
    Set theory—Fiction. | Psychological fiction. | BISAC: FICTION
    / Literary. | FICTION / Family Life. | GSAFD: Domestic fiction.
Classification: LCC PQ7298.417.E73 C6613 2018 | DDC 863/.7—dc23
LC record available at https://lccn.loc.gov/2017030786

IMAGE CREDITS
Map of Argentina on the cover © iStock.com/thepalmer; spiral drawing on the cover and all interior drawings © Verónica Gerber Bicecci.

PRINTED IN THE UNITED STATES OF AMERICA
24 23 22 21 20 19 18 17   1 2 3 4 5 6 7 8

For my brother, Ale, the other half of the empty set.

EMPTY SET

The dossier on my love life is a collection of outsets. A definitively unfinished landscape that stretches over flooded excavations, bare foundations, and ruined structures; an internal necropolis that has been in the early stages of construction for as long as my memory goes back. When you become a collector of beginnings, you can also corroborate, with almost scientific precision, how little variability there is in the endings. I seem to be condemned to renunciation. Although, in fact, there are only minor differences; all the stories end pretty much alike. The sets overlap in more or less the same way, and the only thing that changes is the point you happen to see them from: consensus is the least common option, renunciation is voluntary, but desertion is an imposition.

I have a talent for beginnings. I like that part. The emergency exit, however, is always at hand, so it's also relatively easy for me to leap into the void when something doesn't feel right. To take flight toward nothingness at the least provocation. And that's why this time I don't want any preambles, my collection of outsets is already too large.

I'm tired of preludes, and the only moment it's possible to return to with a modicum of confidence is that finale, the breakup that changed everything in the first place, that turned me into a deserter, a compiler of hopelessly truncated stories.

One fine day, without warning, I woke up at the ending. Hadn't even gotten up when, from the bedroom door, about to leave for one of his classes, Tordo(T) said:

You're not like you used to be.

Spent the rest of the day trying to understand what he meant by that, unable to slip from between the sheets. Just when did I stop being like I used to be?

It all sounded strange, even suspicious.

Thought maybe it had something to do with his midlife crisis. But no. Not long afterwards, it became clear that when someone says, "You're not like you used to be," they actually mean, "I'm in love with someone else."

I broke down. Tordo(T) broke me down.

Almost overnight, I had to pack all my clothes into a suitcase, pick out a few books, write a good-bye letter no one asked me for, call a cab, and return to the only place left for me: Mom(M)'s apartment.

I'd attempted to forget that third floor. Its blocked pipes, disposable plates and cups, the communal sinks on the roof where we sometimes rinsed off the pots and pans, the beat-up domestic appliances, and the cowboy hip tub my Brother(B) and I were so accustomed to, you'd think we lived in another century. I'd stopped thinking about the apartment's unavoidable resemblance to a paleontology lab: the honeycombs of dust; the collection of plant skele-tons mounted on pots; the balls of fluff huddled together to form strange, plush baseboards in the corners; the encrusted grime patterning the walls and ceiling of the kitchen; the gray patina on the windowpanes, produced by infinite layers of dried rain; and the series of strange microorganisms growing in the bottles left standing in the refrigerator.

Even though we could have asked Dad for help, we never got a plumber, never hired anyone to do the cleaning or did it ourselves, because we were sure she'd leave some trace.

We didn't do anything.

The apartment was left suspended in time. Just as it was the day we last saw Mom(M).

In my bedroom, under my old, faithful Humpty Dumpty duvet, it soon became clear that the abruptness of the end-ing had brought things back to the beginning, to some beginning, or at least to the place where they were before Tordo(T). I knew this because, on opening my eyes in the early morning, I heard Mom(M) crossing the hall, speaking aloud in that strange, irascible language I was never able to decipher. My body got up automatically, looked out the bedroom door: the only thing my eyes saw was the bluish light of the computer screen illuminating the hall. She wasn't there.

Late at night, my Brother(B) could always be found in the study. He suffered from insomnia, and it seems to me standing guard was his way of waiting for Mom(M) to reappear. He'd improvised an internet connection from a telephone cable and the passwords the university had given Dad; he was afraid someone would discover that he was duplicating the username, so he only logged on in the small hours. I used to sleep very lightly—it wasn't a matter of waiting up for her, but I'd jump out of bed at the slightest noise. Never asked him, but it seems very likely that my Brother(B) used to hear her too. I followed the light and found him sitting at the computer, surfing the net; it was as if I'd never left, never lived with Tordo(T). Everything was just the same.

You're back, said my Brother(B).

An explanation was unnecessary. Defeat is wordless.

RANGMEBOO

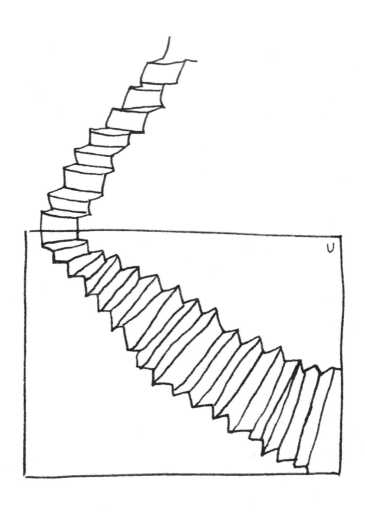

How did we get here, to this point? It all goes back to two days before my fifteenth birthday. Winter 1995. At that time, I was still fourteen and my Brother(B) was seventeen, almost eighteen. It was early in the morning, we were about to leave for school, and Mom(M) said no, said it would be better to stay home. She told us not to turn on the TV, not to turn anything on. She said we had to be silent.

I never had a fifteenth birthday. We'd ordered a bitter chocolate cake for a party that didn't happen. Mom(M)'s interminable absence took away all our birthdays, raveled the passage of time.

There's no recognizable cause, only effects. Correction: only a frontier in space-time, turbulent flows, interrupted. Inter ruptured.

Only a series of scattered, meaningless clues. A set emptying out little by little. Disordered fragments. Correction: shards.

Repetition: winter, 1995.

Mom(M) starts talking about the trees in the park. She says you can see faces in the bark. Says all those faces

are looking toward the house. All those faces are looking at us.

She orders us to stop watering the plants.

If anything should happen to me, she says.

What? my Brother(**B**) and I respond in unison.

. . .

After that, we aren't able to understand what she says.

Or is it that she can't hear us?

What did you say, Mom?

That's how she began to vanish.

And in the end, we couldn't see her anymore.

August 8, 1976

Marisa,

I've decided to change your name. In my diaries, you're called Lina.

The words I've written to you, I've never written to anyone else. They all designate out-of-reach things, except for the reference to your green shoes—which is probably not true—although I haven't forgotten the stomp.

If this was just a word game, I'd go on playing to the end.

Y love you (I wrote "I love you," but added an arm to the I, no matter),

S.

We christened Mom(M)'s apartment "the bunker."

A time capsule where everything is in a state of permanent neglect.

A perfectly closed system Mom(M) constructed before rubbing herself out, one that managed to produce some kind of gravitational singularity.

My Brother(B) started university not long after, and I went to high school. It took Dad years to realize Mom(M) wasn't there—they hadn't spoken since the divorce. At times I'm not completely certain he did realize (or maybe he's much better than us at acting like nothing is wrong). Dad is a methodical man, unlikely to perceive anything outside his routine. He used to phone us once a week—on Thursdays at 2:45 p.m., because that was when he had a few spare moments—and we went to his house for dinner every Sunday. But I guess he must have suspected something, because he always had a manila envelope ready to cover the household expenses and never, ever asked about Mom(M); in part because they'd stopped talking, and in part because the girlfriend of the moment was always there, frowning, wishing Mom(M), my Brother(B), and I didn't exist.

It's not as if we were magicians, we hadn't even agreed upon it; the disappearing act just developed naturally. Not saying anything was enough. It's easy to let others fill the gaps. A sufficiently ambiguous expression can convert someone else's monologue into an imaginary conversation. Silence is a variable that constantly mutates, so it's the other who decides if it's a yes, a no, or any other response.

And anyway: how do you hide something when you don't know where it is?

It's surprising how little it takes to make the whole world believe your life is like everyone else's. In the beginning, they asked us the occasional question, but the fact is no one wanted to know the answers. Then they simply stopped caring, and even if they had asked, we no longer had any answers. No one remembered they hadn't seen Mom(M) for a long time. Oblivion is remorseless; it's memory that settles the accounts, the only evidence of the omission. More than a pair of magicians, we were like those two swindlers in Andersen's tale who pretended to be weavers and designed an invisible outfit for the emperor. We made them believe Mom(M) was there—despite the fact that not even we could see her. She'd crossed a frontier neither my Brother(B) nor I knew how to pass over. We made them believe our daily life was just like that of any other divorced family. The bunker, luckily, never caused any suspicion. It was, in any case, a place no one entered for many years. The space Mom(M) should have occupied was empty; she'd left us part of a hole, and all the rest was outside the visible Universe(U), in an unknown location.

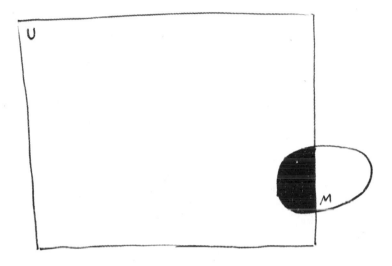

Sneezes and streaming eyes. When they asked me about the purpose of my visit in customs, I opened my mouth, but my voice didn't come out. Had spent the previous ten hours thinking perhaps I'd bought Alonso(A) a ticket on another flight. But no. Considered staying there, sitting in the Buenos Aires airport for a whole week, until my Brother(B) arrived, then taking another flight or a bus to Córdoba. I could stand up to buy juice and a sandwich every so often, somehow ensure no one took my seat during visits to the restroom. It wasn't that many days. But after a few hours of looking at the floor, I decided to go into an office with this sign in the window:

GLACIERS AND THE END OF THE WORLD
FIVE DAYS AND FOUR NIGHTS
ALL INCLUSIVE

Why not? Afterwards, I'd take the bus to Córdoba and arrive at my Grandma(G)'s house the same day as my Brother(B), without a peso in my purse.

The doors of the apartment accumulated more and more bolts. The windows were covered with black canvas. That way we were safe from who knows what.

Have you seen Mom?

No. You?

I look down into the toilet bowl. Maybe the whirlpool had swallowed her up. No.

Did she go out?

No.

From the outside, the bunker is solid, impassible. Inside, it becomes increasingly unstable, unpredictable. Thought I saw her yesterday, I tell my Brother(B) . . . But no. We don't know where she is.

So when was the last time you did see her?

Don't know. You?

Don't know.

Maybe . . .

Maybe what?

We were in the breakfast room.

When?

You had a bowl of cereal.

That could have been any day.

Mom was walking to her chair.

Ah, yes. With a full mug of milky coffee.

Instead of sipping it, she took a whole mouthful and burned her tongue.

No, that was a different day.

It was that same day.

And she spit out the coffee?

Yeah. It splattered as far as the tablecloth. The stains are still there.

Did she say anything?

She made a gesture. Or shouted?

No, the mug slipped out of her hand.

The blue mug?

No, the one somebody gave her a couple years ago.

Ah. The one that says, STILL PERFECT AFTER 40?

Yeah, that's it.

Wonder where they could have bought it.

Don't know. But it's cursed.

The mug?

Yeah.

So did we eventually make it to school that day?

Don't think so.

And the pieces of the mug?

OBSERVATION SHEET III

LOCATION:	Open rooftop.
DATE:	October 1, 2003.
LIGHT POLLUTION (1 10):	7, late.
OBJECT:	Cloud.
SIZE:	Boeing 747.
CONSTELLATION:	Aeroméxico.
LOCAL TIME:	18:30.
DIRECTION:	Unknown.
EQUIPMENT:	Telescope.
FILTER:	No.

OBSERVATION:

NOTES:

I was once obsessed with planes. They seemed the perfect symbol of my family history. Planes have separated us and, at times, brought us back together. A plane is also the nearest thing in existence to a time machine. When I land in Argentina, where my Grandma(G) lives, it always feels like another era, or a previous, scarcely remembered life.

A pair of professional *suspicionists,* that's what we'd become, according to my Brother(B). It was easy for us to believe that events always had a dark side, a shaded area we couldn't make out, one that, despite being empty, always meant something more. People often say things aren't just black or white; I'm not so sure. The white and the black are nothing more than a question of light, of totality and absence of light. The black is hollowness and the white fullness, or at least that's what they taught us at art school. Whatever. The fact is that the things we can't see don't hide themselves in the shades of gray, or in the white or black, but on the fine line separating those two totalities. A place we can't even imagine, a horizon of no return. It's at the boundaries that everything becomes invisible. There are things, I'm sure, that can't be told in words. There are things that only occur between the white and the black, and very few people can see them. Something like that happened with Mom(M): an optical illusion, an inexplicable mystery of matter. And also with Tordo(T), although, in his case, reconstructing the sequence was relatively easy.

The last thing he said to me was:

Something broke, I don't know exactly what, but we can't go on together any longer.

He didn't know what had broken?

But (I) needed to find out.

So (I) went back over the sequence of events again and again, cut minutes here and there, and ended up realizing what was obvious: we're constantly drawing something we can never manage to see completely. We only have one side, an edge of our own history, and the rest is hidden. It's not worth the effort to recount the details of the breakup, but the process was more or less like this:

Once upon a time there was an intersection called IT

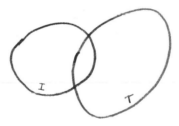

Suddenly, in the IT intersection, a void appears

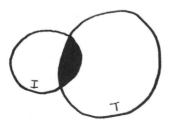

In fact, the void is a symptom of intersection TH, which I can't see

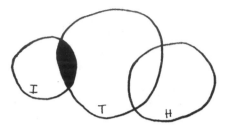

Then T moves away with H, and I is left with the hole

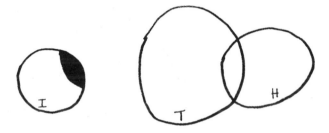

I am I, Tordo is T, and H is Her.

Conclusion: Nobody else was broken, and it's not clear to me if (I) still carry the hole or am missing a piece.

Judging character from a portrait seems like a bad idea to me. People do it all the time, and it's unfair: no one likes who they are in photographs. But as I didn't know him, and was wrapped up in his mother's things, there was no getting away from it. From my point of view, Alonso(A) was dulled by Marisa(M_x)'s outfit and movie-star pose, as if all he could do was bow his head or cover his face with his hair.

There was a long, solitary period ahead of me in the old bunker. My Brother(B) moved out to live with his girl-friend the same week I returned. Helped him take some boxes of books and records, two suitcases of clothes, and his pillow over to the other apartment. We made a couple of trips on foot; it was just a few blocks. In the bunker, there were bits of furniture full of useless objects—all with a frosting of dust, as if Popocatépetl's fumarole had thrown out all its ash there—but he didn't want to take any of them with him. Seven years had gone by, yet we were still trying to keep the spell intact, even though we weren't sure exactly what that spell was. My first night alone, I heard her talking in the living room again. There was no com-puter to light the way, so used the walls as my guide. No one. Went back to bed.

Needed to find something to do. Anything at all.

It was that or go crazy.

After an exhaustive reconnaissance, I decided that, of all the problems in Mom(M)'s apartment, the most worry-ing was the damp seeping through the main wall of the living room, because it meant one flank of the bunker was going soft. The wall was swelling, the paint forming bubbles you could burst with a finger. The exterior was forcing the interior to give way. Didn't want the bunker to suck me in permanently, but neither could I, after so long, allow the system collapse. Got up the next day with the firm intention of solving the problem, found the number of a timber supplier in the *Yellow Pages*, and ordered three pine plywood boards—48 × 96 inches, and half an inch thick—to cover and reinforce the wall. The boards arrived in no time at all and had to be hoisted up onto the balcony, as they didn't fit through the door. I cleared a space on the living room floor and spent several days sanding, applying wood fill, and then sanding again to completely smooth the imperfections. Sawdust accumulated over the layer of dust on the furniture. When that task was finished, I stood looking at the boards as if they were a blank canvas, though the surface wasn't completely empty. The grain of the wood made a pattern. Some lines were thicker than my little finger, others much finer. Ran my index finger along one that was exactly its width. It didn't take much thought, all that was needed was to fill a given form without exceeding its boundaries; it was a retired lady's pastime, but implied almost Zen levels of concentration that might help me kill time. I had a little black and white paint—two "non-colors"—and their possible blends.

Mom(M) used to call Dad "Lito" when she was feeling affectionate. She once said it was his revolutionary name. Dad said he wasn't a revolutionary, didn't have a code name, and had only handed out flyers in factories. In my family, everyone contradicts everyone else, and in the end, the only things left are holes. Worse still: nobody ever wants to talk about the holes. In elementary school, I learned about my "nuclear family," the one that lives in Mexico, and that idea seemed plausible because I could imagine an explosion that had scattered us all around the world. That bomb, in our case, is called dictatorship. And the explosion, exile. Mom(M) also confessed that Dad was on the black list, and then indignantly said everyone was on the black list. And there it ended. The things we heard came to us like that, in a disordered way, piles of disconnected anecdotes that were just pure chaos in my head.

October 18

Solona,
I ma nningpla a pirt ot Natigenar ni Bercemde
D'I ekil uoy ot emoc oot. Woh bouta ti?
V.

He didn't answer.

Tordo(T) is a visual artist, but he would have preferred to be a writer. He used to invent a new name for me every day, as if trying out characters on me. Sometimes he'd also attempt to find some likeness between me and the actresses in the movies we watched together; he always discovered something, some detail. I, on the other hand, wanted to be a visual artist, but visualized almost everything in words. My fellow students at art school used to tell me that was really weird.

The day I took Tordo(T) to the airport, he flaunted the tattoo he'd just had done in the famous parlor of a "Doctor" somebody or other. I didn't know the place and had never heard of the tattoo artist, but didn't say so. He lifted the gauze with a hint of arrogance; the area was still inflamed, and there were traces of dried blood. It was a bird's-eye view of him halfway across a high-wire. He'd had himself tattooed on his shoulder! It should have been my cue to take to my heels. I didn't. That tautological (had just learned that concept at university) gesture seemed brilliant. Later, naturally, it didn't. Whatever the case, I was concerned by the metaphor of him walking a tightrope just at the time he started dating me, but it was more disturbing that there were two Tordos(T) in the same body. The tattoo might have been a portent I couldn't see: he did indeed end up splitting himself in two. Not sure . . . perhaps I was attracted by the idea of waiting for him at one end of the wire, and him deciding to walk toward me. It's obvious I wasn't seeing things clearly because he eventually went in the opposite direction.

Two Universes(U).

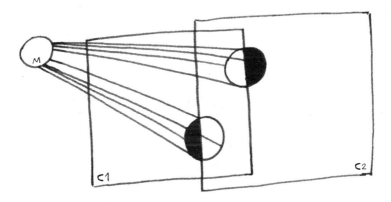

Or rather, two countries: Argentina(c_1), Mexico(c_2).
And Mom(M).

Maybe if we learned to be in two places at the same time.

Mom(M) found a way to be right in the middle, in a place where no one could find her.

To forget someone, you have to be extremely methodical. Falling out of love is a sort of illness that can only be fought off with routine. This hadn't occurred to me before—it was my survival instinct that discovered it. So I started searching for activities and time-tabling them. Spent the whole morning lying facedown on the huge plywood board, following the line of a grain with a brush dipped in black, white, or gray. Two or three grain lines a day, no more. A fourth, and my hand would begin to tremble and overstep the mark. Sometimes had to use an ultrafine brush, sometimes a thicker one. It was, above all, an exercise in patience.

While painting, I remembered my freshman-year sculpture teacher from La Esmeralda art school. He was Japanese. The twenty-five years he'd spent in Mexico hadn't done him much good, because he spoke Spanish as if he'd just arrived; that is, he hardly spoke it at all. His greatest aesthetic concern was that we understood the cycle of life. For our first class, he took us on the subway to buy four hens at La Merced market. Then we held a pagan christening rite, during which we named them Klein, Fontana, Manzoni, and Beuys. They lived that whole semester in a huge cage in the studio. We used to take them out to get some fresh air in the school courtyards twice a week, there was a roster for feeding them posted on the board. Some students—who knows why—came to feel a fondness for them. At the end of the semester, Mifusama Suhomi turned up with a gigantic cooking pot and a load of coal, saying we had to kill the birds. There was a vast silence. He himself wrung their necks, and we all helped pluck them. He made a soup we had to consume to complete the cycle. Life-death-life, he said. No other soup has ever compared to that one. Don't know how good an artist he was, but he had the makings of a great chef. And although his Spanish was feeble, he used the words accurately, as a sensei would. Two words alone were enough to convey something as essential and complex as the fact that things begin, then end, and then begin again.

His classes were as strange as they come: he demonstrated what plaster is instead of teaching us how to use it to make molds and casts. Explained where marble came from, instead of giving us hammers and chisels. The same happened with wood: To make plywood board, tree turn in enormous pencil sharpener, then big press squash tree shavings. I learned that the grain of the wood tells a detailed story of the tree's experiences during a specific period. It all sounded pleasantly credible: that each line of the grain of my pine plywood boards told me a different story, and that saved me from having to think about my own. The area of each grain line corresponds to a ring in the trunk, and each ring can correspond, although not exactly, to a year in the life of the tree. I later discovered there's a science for all that: dendrochronology. The age of the trunk can be calculated by following the radial growth of the rings traced on it from the center outward. Dendrochronology appealed to me as a career. But you can't see the age of a tree on pine plywood boards. The enormous rotating pencil sharpener slices through the trunk at an angle. This diagonal cut disorders everything: each wood shaving contains discontinuous moments from the life of the tree, not a linear, much less a concentric, chronology.

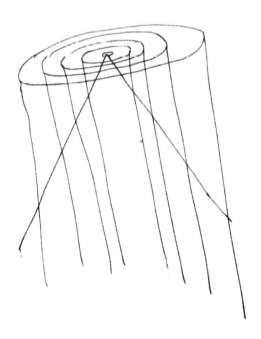

Mifusama Suhomi gave us each a pencil and a sharpener. After a couple of false starts, he said: Perfect shavings, now you. Something very similar to that conical shaving is what is compressed and layered to make a plywood board. In the bunker, there were three wooden panels with time disordered and overlapping. If only that were possible: to disorder time. I'd like to invent a science that investigates how a pine plywood board disorders time. It would be useful to relocate the moments when certain things happen, to put the endings at the beginnings, for instance (or anywhere else). Or the past in a future so distant we never reach the moment of confronting it. The mornings would slip by in such reflections.

In an inner dialogue all the words return like boomerangs.

Did he have a girlfriend? Inner cataclysm. After dinner, Alonso(**A**) would rise from the table and leave me there with a promise to return, but he always took too long, and I always ended up going home before he came back. Thought at first he must be using the bathroom, but later realized he was shutting himself in there to speak on the telephone. Plucked up my courage and asked Chema what Alonso(**A**)'s girlfriend was called. Mayra(**M**ᵧ) with a *y*, he replied, smiling. Had hoped for a different response and so felt sad and bad, but didn't show it. Alonso(**A**) and I used to tell each other many things, but he hadn't said anything about Mayra(**M**ᵧ).

This is what (**I**) thought:

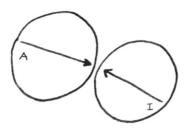

But reality is tough:

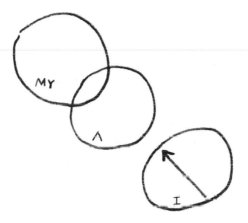

Violeta had been my friend since elementary school, and she was one of the few people I spoke to during those months. She was auditing a class at UNAM that was directly related to her thesis topic. She also spent a lot of time in the Main Library, studying for an intensive Chinese course offered by the modern languages department; she'd gotten the idea of doing a master's there, but it was going to take her four years just to learn Mandarin. She invited me to go to the library with her in the afternoons because she was worried about me. Had nothing better to do at that time of day, so accepted the invitation.

She did the talking—I didn't feel up to it—but even then, she'd manage to convert my silence into something pleasant. How did she put up with me? Sometimes her boyfriend came with us too. That was convenient, because it saved me from feeling guilty about not talking. He went to the Aesthetics Library, where he was analyzing a Mixtec or Zapotec (not really certain which) codex for his bachelor's thesis. When he joined us later, they used to discuss me. I'd nod, but hardly understood a word of it; suddenly "my situation" had become a pretext for talking about other problems, ones that weren't exactly mine.

Spent my first visits to the library leafing through books, mooching around the corridors, walking the building from top to bottom, convinced that I'd find something, although not quite certain what. In fact, I spent the time imagining a reunion with Tordo(T), imagining he'd repented and come looking for me; going over and over the scene in which he steered me to some out-of-the-way shelving unit and cornered me there, where we couldn't be seen. There was no need to invent a reason for his being in the Main Library, or an explanation for how he knew he'd cross paths with me there. What was important was the reconciliation. These things happen when you've got nothing to do. Then I began to lose hope. Well, in fact, I decided that the reunion (of course it never happened) would lack all spontaneity if every single detail of it already existed in my imagination.

It finally occurred to me to look up hypothetical titles in the library catalog. Perhaps someone had already written about everything I needed to know at that moment: *On the Analysis of Time in a Pine Plywood Board, Depictions of Time in Wood, Grain Lines and Time: A Theory of Chaos* and other such combinations that, naturally, didn't yield any results.

When an event is inexplicable, a hole is created some-where. So we are full of holes, like Swiss cheese. Holes inside holes.

A postcard next to my bowl of soup:

Chema had already gotten into the habit of setting a place for me at the table, so I went down at two thirty on the dot. Alonso(A) would usually be there at that hour, taking the lids off the pots and pans while chatting to me about what he'd done during the day. It was an invitation to an event at the Museo Tamayo with a pompous title—*The Poetics of the Illegible: Dysgraphia, Hypergraphia, Lettrism and other Twentieth-Century Visual Writings*— and was addressed to Marisa(M_x). Despite the fact that the title was so pretentious and had a subtitle more suited to a doctoral thesis, the idea of attending appealed to me. As he hadn't turned up for lunch on that particular day, it wasn't clear whether Alonso(A) was inviting me to go with him or not. Just in case, I took the postcard with me, supposing that was the best way to communicate my intention of accompanying him.

My schedule was simple: work on my plywood board in the mornings, meet up with Violeta in the afternoons. Sundays were still dinner at Dad's. But Saturdays were dangerous because there was no fixed routine. The first Saturday I decided to leave the house, I ran into Tordo(T). Several weeks, perhaps months, had gone by since I'd moved out. My presence brought the triangle diagram into the visible spectrum, even though Tordo(T) denied that figure's existence. They used to call me sometimes from a small gallery in the Condesa neighborhood with a request to do the exhibition photography. Guess it was cheaper to employ me—an absolute amateur—than to get a professional with the necessary equipment. I arrived early, set up my tripod, and started shooting; the place was empty. Tordo(T) knew perfectly well I'd be taking the photos at some point because he was the one who got the job for me. After a while I turned around, and there they were, coming through the door arm in arm like two people who have spent their whole lives together. There should be a three-line space here. It seems to me that particular formatting could contain a moment of high tension: three and a half blank lines. But that would be giving it undue importance.

Unlike me, photography was Her(H) profession. And from the moment they first met, Tordo(T) never stopped going on about Her(H). That was suspicious, but I didn't make the connection. It's still not clear to me how a "Someone stole her camera, but she didn't turn a hair, just went on dancing" or "I'm not completely sure about her visual discourse, she's an opportunist" could give rise to mistrust. So it didn't, until that very instant when the two of them were there, across the room, and it dawned on me that he'd never directly introduced us, just pointed Her(H) out from a distance. And it was odd when Tordo(T) insisted, "The haircut she had in that video was really ugly." It should have made me suspicious that a woman who clearly wasn't should "look ugly," but apparently, for the first time in my life, I wasn't being a *suspicionist*, and was incapable of seeing the wood for the trees. That's the most awful part of it: something so obvious wasn't.

We have to accept—wanted to say to them as an ice-breaker, but no words came out of my mouth—that if we join the distances between us with straight lines, the result would be more like a triangle than any other figure. The three of us are there, paralyzed. I had time to analyze and measure; it was an isosceles triangle, but slightly deformed: the side joining them was much shorter than the ones they shared with me. Guess that's the way it always is. Hi, hi. Good-bye, good-bye. They go off set and I just stand there, rooted to the spot, like a tree. The triangle stretches out and out and out, but doesn't snap.

I roundly refuse to form a part of the triangular configuration they imposed on me. Prefer to think of myself as a cone; some people say a cone is a rotating triangle, even better. A cone can also be a series of circles tapering from large to small, with the smallest being just a dot. Or a perfect time shaving. So the map of the situation, or rather, the Universe(U) in which (I) was trapped, could be seen differently. What's left of me could also look like a slice of pie. Tordo(T) and Her(H), they're just triangles:

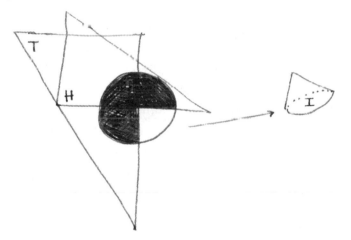

After that encounter, it occurred to me to type just one keyword into the library catalog: *triangle*. A book in English appeared: *How Can a Triangle Be Cut?* It seemed like fate—the title was exactly what I needed. But the basis of all the solutions to cutting triangles in that text, in addition to being impossible, resulted in other triangles. Wasn't completely sure just what I was looking for, but did know more triangles weren't the solution to my triangle problem.

"If only telescopes didn't just look toward the sky, but were able to pierce the earth so we could find them . . ." says a woman with a small spade in her hand, walking around in the middle of the Atacama Desert. That's how the documentary film my Brother(B) and I saw at a small theater starts. She and a number of others have spent decades looking for the bodies of their disappeared. There are enormous telescopes in the Atacama Desert that see and hear what happens in the rest of the Universe(U), see and hear what we can't see or hear.

This, for example, is how Earth would look from Jupiter through a telescope.

(Maybe even smaller.)

Those women have found traces of calcium from the bones of their dead. Astronomers, on the other hand, measure the calcium in the stars. We (my Brother(B) and I) have other kinds of problems with calcium: empty milk cartons neither of us have drunk from, pieces of cheese that disappear from the refrigerator without having been tasted.

This is more or less how the stars look from Earth on a clear night:

The whole Universe(U), even time, is made up of the same material.

From a plane, a person would look smaller than this (or maybe not look like anything at all):

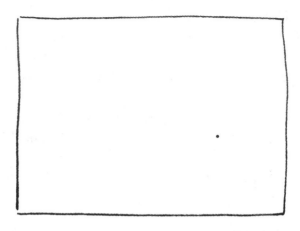

The body of her husband, or at least the remains of his calcium, is there, and that woman knows it. But it's like knowing nothing, because the Atacama Desert is vast.

Several people would look smaller than this from a plane:

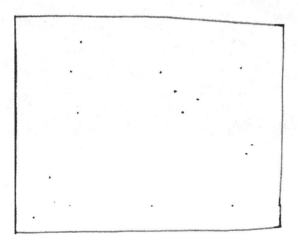

Astronomers don't know much either, that's why they build telescopes.

It's said every answer to a question is a new question. That too is something uniting us: neither astronomers, nor those searching for the disappeared, nor my Brother(B), nor I know anything. We're all trying to find traces, or asking ourselves questions.

We're all waiting for what we can't see to finally appear.

Here's where this story ends.

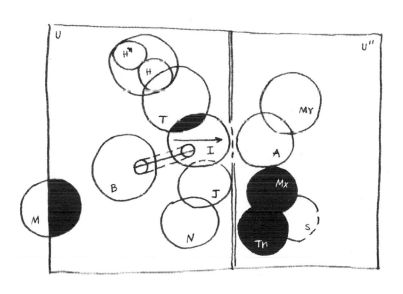

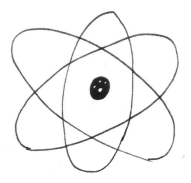

Typed *cone* into the library catalog the next week, and chose one book, *Shadow Cone,* and two articles: "Calculation of the Thickness of a Worm Gear Derived from the Cone" and "A Historical Reconstruction of the Quaternary Period in the Vegetation of the Southern Cone of America: An Interdisciplinary Approach." The poems in the first were an immediate disappointment. Closed my eyes, picked out a page at random, and ran my finger down to:

> *Place this line on the precise dot*
> *and we'll make love in Morse code.*

Laughed aloud and the book fell to the floor; a couple of people turned their heads, but no one seemed annoyed. The second text had diagrams and a lot of formulas; spent quite a while studying them, hoping to understand all those numbers, letters, brackets, and signs, but couldn't. I did manage to deduce that the "worm" of a gear refers to the serpentine engravings on the screw. In other words, it's what makes it different from a nail and—not so sure about this—the cone is the head of the screw. In any case, there was no point in attempting to understand it all. The third text was from a journal of biology. There, for the first time, was a mention of my secret vocation: the keyword, *dendrochronology*. I smiled. No, that's not true. Went to look up *dendrochronology* in a dictionary, and that's when I smiled.

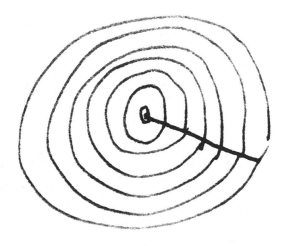

Based on that finding, it seemed a good idea to work in the Biology Institute Library. Guess Violeta and her boyfriend didn't quite understand how I ended up there, since my major had been visual arts, but they went along with it, because, from their very personal point of view, the important thing was "supporting me." I didn't completely understand why I was there. What I wanted to research was the idea of time on the pine plywood boards, to find a way of understanding how it is transformed in the grain and conical sections. Dendrochronology was a means of studying time and space without going up in a rocket or solving quantum physics equations. Curiously enough, it was an astronomer who discovered the language of trees. Like me, Andrew Ellicott Douglass had strayed off the path. He'd been working on sunspots but ended up studying tree rings to see if they could tell him anything about the sun. It's not only a matter of knowing the age of trees: the history of the forests where they lived is recorded in the designs in the wood. The trees retain scars from fires and every sort of natural disaster: earthquakes, hurricanes, diseases. Insects also leave their mark. You can even check the age of a violin or a piece of furniture by counting the number of rings in the wood. A trunk is the logbook of the ecosystem. And cutting down a forest isn't just an ecological tragedy; it is, quite literally, the destruction of an archive of historical data. But trees write in a language that can't be seen. Wonder what my life would look like inside a tree trunk, what all those lines, knots, and circumferences would mean.

Wonder how a set of truncated outsets, an abrupt ending, or a disappearance would be written in that language.

September 12, 1976

Marisa,

Every twenty minutes I ask myself if something will come from you in the post. Aren't you going to write me letters anymore? It's fifty thousand years since your last one. No matter. I've already told you: if you don't want to write to me, don't. But I have a right to tell you about certain things I do, like keeping time in reverse, not for the days that have passed, but for the ones left (until I see you, of course).

Shall I go on waiting for some sign of life, or turn up at your house uninvited?

S.

On the other side of the park—the one the bunker overlooks—there was going to be a party. Ana had invited me and I only went along because there was no good excuse for not crossing that green space. Ana was a schoolmate of my Brother(в), but she was also my friend, and had invited me to the party because of my recently acquired single status and, of course, hers. In any case, we really only entered the building together, and after that she went off the radar. It was a kind of international hostel that had notices with instructions in English all over the place: above the kitchen sink, in the bathroom, on the refrigerator, on the living room table. There was an enormous calendar showing the days for cleaning, the roster for taking out the trash and using the washing machine, payment dates . . . things I'd only ever seen in TV series, and that made my routine feel far too basic. One last notice—decidedly temporary—was hanging in the yard:

¡BIENVENIDOS! / WELCOME! / WILLKOMMEN!
ANDREAS AND JÜRGEN

Two new German guys staying in the house, doing internships at the architecture firm where Ana worked. I liked his name: Jürgen(J). He was tall, taller than me, unlike Tordo(T). We just stood there next to each other the entire evening: Ana had kidnapped Andreas, his only friend, and neither of us knew anyone else; he couldn't speak Spanish and I didn't feel like talking to him in English. Each time I finished my wine, Jürgen(J) went to find the bottle and refilled my glass. I smiled at him, he smiled at me. The only thing I said to him all night was: Where's your room? We went up the main staircase, then a smaller spiral one, and along a very narrow corridor with several doors. His was the last. On the way, my head began to spin. His luggage still hadn't been unpacked. While he took off his shirt and shoes, I examined the oddments other residents had left on the shelves. He came up behind me and kissed my neck. I reached back, undid his zipper, and put one hand inside his boxers. He murmured something in German in my ear. Then he turned me around so we were facing each other, lifted me high up in the air—as I descended, my skirt billowed out; that instant was chiseled in my mind for days—and backed me against the wall. And that was it. He didn't know my name and I couldn't speak his language. Afterwards, we lay down on the bed. He fell asleep, I stared at the ceiling for a long time.

From a *Lonely Planet Mexico* thrown on the floor beside the pillow, a piece of a face peeked out. In the part hidden inside the guidebook, he was kissing that face. Written on the reverse of the photograph was a pretty recent date and something else; didn't know what. I could make out the signature—Nadia(N)—but didn't feel anything. No, that's not quite right—in fact I did feel something, something strange. Not jealousy, just a sensation of disappearing; my body was becoming transparent. I didn't exist there, because in that place, I definitively did not exist. And in fact that wasn't a problem, because I didn't want to exist there, what bothered me was not being able to exist anywhere. Thought about Jürgen(J)'s luggage. His two enormous suitcases full of things he had nowhere to put. Also thought about the "luggage" I'd carried into his life that night. We were two strangers helping each other cross the street.

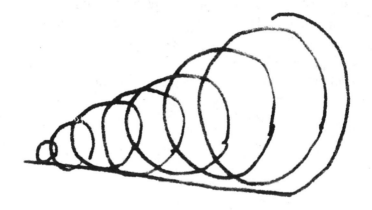

Woke feeling guilty—most likely due to the wine—and spent the whole morning finding ways to stop myself from phoning Tordo(T). Decided to unpack suitcases and boxes, only to end up dialing his cell phone number from memory. He answered without preamble:

What's wrong?

Hi . . . How are you?

Fine. What's wrong?

Just beginning to realize I forgot some things and . . .

Why didn't you take all your stuff? No one was hassling you.

Not sure, Tordo. I packed up two years in an hour and . . .

You can't come here. Tell me what you're missing, and I'll take it somewhere for you to pick up.

Think I insulted him. Then hung up without saying good-bye.

Looked toward Mom(M)'s room at the end of the passage. The door was shut. How could Tordo(T) refuse to allow me into my own home?! Maybe it wasn't my home any longer . . . Opened the door. Maybe he wasn't my home any longer. Looking for the remote on her night table, saw a sheet of notepaper with a message, written in fountain pen, in her handwriting:

Love confirms the circularity of the universe

There was no period at the end, and there were some roundish doodles in the bottom corner, as if she'd been trying out the pen or had become lost in thought. Her story, like that phrase, had been left in suspense. The sheet of paper was weighted down with a limestone pebble I'd brought back from camp for her. It was the finest piece in a collection of finds I'd been amassing since childhood: gray, just like any other, but with a white line of silica that formed a perfect circle. Lay there studying the document for the rest of the day, with the noise of the television in the background. Couldn't understand what she wanted to say.

Hardly anything was visible:

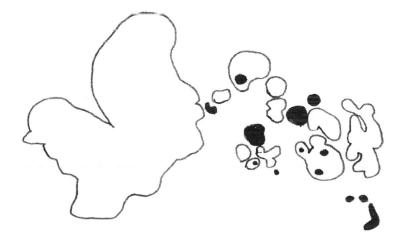

The telescope was in Marisa(M_x)'s bathroom, and the only thing you could point it at was the opposite wall. Would have preferred to view stars and planets but got used to the fissures and cracks in the wall; sometimes looked for possible constellations there, black holes and life forms:

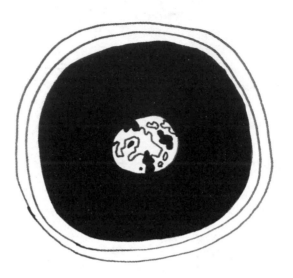

Verónica Gerber Bicecci

There are one hundred thirteen grain lines on the first pine plywood board: I counted them. After filling in seventy-three (in no particular order), a sort of map starts to become visible: lines, islands, and knots. Sometimes the enormous panels lying on the floor also make me think of the ocean: maybe because the grays, whites, and blacks suddenly turned slightly blue. That happens to some paints—the black releases an almost imperceptible bluish hue. Mom(M) said she first saw the sea at the age of nineteen, when she went on a trip to Mar del Plata with some girlfriends. If it was possible, right now Mom(M) would be living in a shack on the seashore in some remote place. When she was annoyed or fed up with us, she used to threaten one of two things: "I'm going to give you away to the Gypsies" or "One fine day I'll go to the end of the world where no one can find me." Perhaps she'd kept her promise.

If I'd been able to choose the city of my birth, it would have been Garabato, a commune of the province of Santa Fe, Argentina. Never been there, but would love to be able to say I was a Doodler: an inhabitant of, as its name in Spanish suggests, a badly drawn, illegible town.

My Brother(B) comes to visit the bunker. He's cradling a black kitten, only a few weeks old. Later, the doorman tells me there are six more of the little creatures in the middle of the park, and that a neighbor is trying to find them homes; but this kitten, the seventh, has set out to find her own. She had crossed the park and the street and curled up in a flowerpot by the door of my building to enjoy the sun. When he put her down on the floor, she immediately went prowling around the paint pots and accidentally let her tail fall in the white. The stain didn't come out for days. My Brother(B) stood for quite a while, inspecting the boards. The second one was, by then, in progress.

Still haven't found a job, right?

What to say? Immersed in my research, I hadn't even looked for one. There was no point in telling him about time and cones, much less showing him how one of the walls of the bunker had gone soft and explaining how I was going to solve the problem. Didn't tell him about the note in Mom(M)'s bedroom either.

We should go to Argentina, he says out of the blue (still looking at the boards).

Where'd that idea come from? I eventually reply (apparently they produce a sort of trance-like effect).

Don't know, it just occurred to me . . .

When? (like a mandala).

In December?

I'm in (but without colors).

And how are you going to pay for the flight when you haven't got anything coming in?

Didn't answer. I'd get the money somehow.

Tordo(T) wasn't going to call. He hadn't called after we kissed for the first time either. Damnit. Promised myself not to think about the beginning. But, in fact, that wasn't the only beginning. Our story began several times and only ended once, that's why it's impossible to understand which of the beginnings was the one that ended. I waited a few weeks, but zilch. Then wrote a note and carried it with me until we both turned up at the same exhibition opening and it was possible to hand it to him in person. Would rather not try to remember what it said; I was nineteen, the year 2000 was about to come to an end, and I was madly in love after one kiss (he was drunk), that seems a sufficient explanation. He didn't reach out after the note either. When I asked him why, he said it was complicated. It always seemed to me Tordo(T) was afraid. I was. But the complication was that he was in the middle of divorce proceedings.

The next time we met was at a party thrown by his students early the following semester; he told me he was going to New York for a while. A lump formed in my throat.

Offered to give him a ride home, and when we were saying good-night, he said he'd really liked my note, and, once again, put his lips to mine; he slipped his hand under my blouse, and then his tongue between my teeth. Tordo(T) lived in a small studio apartment; you had to wind your way around packing cases to get anywhere. The bed was completely covered in notebooks; we cleared a space by throwing them on the floor. It was true, he was leaving, he was very nearly ready to go. It seemed the story, yet again, was not going to begin.

Slept without pajamas for the first time in my life that night. In the morning, I put a pan of water on the electric stove, made tea, and then went back to the bed with a cup in each hand. Tordo(T) had been watching me. I felt embarrassed, spilled the better part of the tea on the pillow then hid myself under the sheets. Tordo(T) uncovered my head and ran his fingers through my hair.

Why don't you come with me?

My body started trembling inside.

Impossible to answer that question, and not long afterwards, I left.

But that evening I sought him out again, said yes, and drove him to the airport. It was at that precise moment, in the departures area, when he flaunted his new tattoo. He left, and then nada. In his letters, Tordo(T) said he was waiting for me. I flew out that summer.

During the entire cab ride from JFK to Brooklyn, I lay on his lap, only able to see bits of bridges, the sky, and the odd traffic signal. Tordo(T) told me he wanted to introduce me to some friends and that he'd arranged to meet them later in a bar. Imagined for a moment the scene in which they wouldn't let me in because I was under twenty-one. Words failed me; it was obvious I wasn't old enough to live the life I was living.

We went up the stairs to the second floor; Tordo(T) carried my suitcase in one hand and somehow managed to get the other between my legs. As soon as we'd gotten through the door, we went straight to bed. For me, this was the third beginning with Tordo(T). When (I) felt him inside me, the tears began to flow uncontrollably, like a child's. Had never before been so terrified, but still didn't want to be anywhere else in the world but there with him. We came at the same time (IT) and hugged each other very tightly. Those were the only kinds of signs (I) could see around that time:

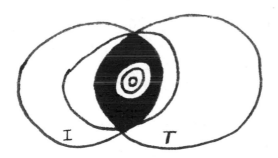

My Brother(B)'s girlfriend offered me a job she didn't have time for, but would have loved to take on. Something about organizing an archive and the personal effects of a writer. The name? Marisa(M_x) Chubut. Never heard of her. She'd set up an appointment for me, so I could begin as soon as possible. It was my Brother(B)'s idea; she didn't say so, but the plan had his stamp. With my pay, it would be possible, for example, to buy a ticket to Argentina. There was nothing for me to do but agree. The problem was finding the courage to leave the bunker. Venturing out on a new route implied encountering Her(H) again and again. Her(H), as may be clear by now, was Tordo(T)'s new girlfriend. And Her(H^*)—this has yet to be explained—face was on hundreds of billboards of every variety. Even worse, Her(H^*) voice could be heard on the radio and at all the pirated CD stands, not to mention the appearances in movie commercials and on television. It was a nightmare for me, although everyone else in the world thought Her(H^*) brilliant. In fact, it was not Her(H) that was famous, the face on the billboards was an identical twin: (H^*) was an actress in the new-wave telenovelas with "social criticism" who went on to have a career as a singer. Her(H*) fame was so vast that a reggaeton version of one of Her(H*) songs was made for a Bubu Lubu commercial.

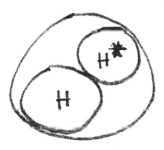

Going to the movies, watching TV, listening to the radio, or driving along major avenues were all high-risk activities, as they could involve coming across Them(H, H*). Perhaps this synthesis was unfair: for a long time I thought of Them(H, H*) as the same person because their duplicated image added an unbearable weight to the void facing me. The downside, among other dumb things, was that I had to stop eating Bubu Lubus.

Her(H*) face was impossible to escape, but even so, Tordo and Her(H) had managed to stay under the radar. Had everyone known but me? That was the problem with going out: my brain unleashed a torrent of venomous associations. Told my Brother(B)'s girlfriend I'd take the job, then called Violeta later to give her the news: she was pleased, but not so happy when she realized I wouldn't be going to the university with her anymore. Without thinking about it any further, I got into my mother's '90 Tsuru. It was difficult to find a route in which Their(H, H^*) smile didn't suddenly appear around a corner. The upper level of the Periférico beltway would be a lousy idea, because from there the billboards were unmissable, so I opted to travel below with the radio off, the windows up, and a vista limited to dozens of columns and a stretch of concrete.

If the planets continue to move in their orbits, maybe Alonso(A) and I will manage to coincide at some point.

Set up the telescope on the balcony of the bunker, facing the park, and stayed there with Nuar to watch the people walking their dogs or running the perimeter. It was pretty monotonous. There were whole days when nothing happened. It's hard for anything important to occur when you don't know what you expect. There are things that can be seen with the naked eye, of course, but with a telescope I can make out details that would otherwise pass unnoticed. My favorite thing about the observations is that there's no sound. Everything that happens out there is silence from in here. Except, perhaps, the birdsong, which I can't understand. It drives Nuar crazy.

Have you come to clear out the señora's stuff?

To do the archiving, yeah.

His name was Chema, and he was the faithful assistant and caretaker of the house. He took me to the third floor, unlocked a door, put the key in my hand, and vanished.

Inside, it was completely silent. Marisa(M_x) Chubut's bedroom was also a carefully decorated studio. An enormous window looked out onto the garden, a piece of cloth with Moorish motifs hung above the head of the bed, and the furniture seemed to have been passed down through generations. There was a selection of first editions of Mexican and Argentinian literature in a museum case; also recognized an original Joy Laville painting and a Toledo print. It was nothing like the bunker, which was the typical apartment of seventies exiles, with pieces of furniture in the "Mexican rustic" style, others of imitation wood, a bookcase of cheap editions, the Salvat encyclopedia, melamine crockery, and reproductions of the grand masters of painting (Vermeer, van Gogh) hanging on the walls. Sat in a small armchair to wait, and after a while Chema returned.

Señor Alonso is going to be late getting home. He says it'd be better if you came back next week.

Señor Alonso? Who's he?

The señora's son.

Ah.

Told my Brother(B)'s girlfriend about what had happened, not hiding my annoyance at having to wait until the following week to go back because her friend Alonso(A) hadn't turned up for the appointment. And what's more, it was weird wandering around the bedroom of someone I didn't know and hadn't realized was dead, even if that was supposedly obvious. I know very little, almost nothing, about death. Death is another kind of absence, one that leaves a sudden, big (enormous) wound that gradually heals, or so it seems to me. Disappearance, on the other hand, makes a tiny, uncertain wound that grows a little larger every day. (My Brother(B) and I thought up the theory of wounds during the many empty hours in the bunker.)

I collided with a parallel Universe(U^{II}) that, lucky for me, gave signs of being an emergency exit. Marisa(M_x)'s funeral was just a few months ago, my Brother(B)'s girlfriend said in explanation, and Alonso(A) hasn't been able to sort out all her papers, he's really busy, and all that must be hard for him.

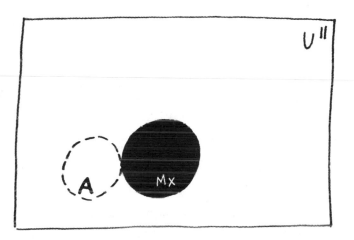

One afternoon, having forgotten we were neighbors, I saw Jürgen(J) crossing the park and went down to "run into him." It felt good to me that he didn't ask my name, that he believed I didn't speak English, that we had nothing to say to each other. And best of all: that we wouldn't need many words to get to his room. Our relationship was about other things. It was a matter of balance, or rather, it functioned as a counterpoise to an equilibrium in which (I) was the fulcrum:

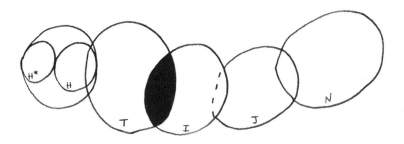

His handwriting interested me, it was big and scrawly, difficult to decipher. The legs of the p and the y were longer than the others, and the A of his name occupied a lot of space at the bottom of the page. He gave me a set of very odd instructions:

> Dear Verónica,
>
> Start by gathering the photos together, they're all over the place, but mostly in the chest of drawers. Throw out the blurred ones with no people in them, the unidentifiable landscapes . . . There's no point in keeping those. Then you can put them in the folders and binders I've bought. If you finish before I come back, start emptying the desk and classifying the documents and other stuff.
>
> I hope to meet you soon,
>
> Alonso

Wanted to meet him too, even if he had stood me up again.

The chest of drawers did indeed contain photographs, but also postcards, clippings, diplomas, and other stuff. My first task was to organize them into sets: assorted papers in one pile, postcards used for correspondence in another, unused postcards in a third. The heaps of photographs, classified by format, gradually traced the different eras of Marisa(M_x)'s life: her forebears in sepia, her infancy in tiny black-and-white reproductions, squarer ones with pale colors corresponding to her youth, magenta-tinged rectangular ones from her middle-age, eighties minilab images, home prints from the nineties, and so on. I made a time line across the whole room, and in doing so, realized Alonso(A)'s childhood seemed very much like my Brother(B)'s, despite the difference in their ages. Or maybe all family portraits are the same. What distinguished them was Marisa(M_x) Chubut, who dressed like an old-time movie actress, and not all moms look like that on weekdays; it gave her a rather bizarre air. By contrast, the bunker's family album was on indefinite pause; if anyone saw it today, they'd think our camera had been stolen or that we'd all died in a tragic accident because it comes to a halt so abruptly. The last photos I remember are from Cuernavaca, in the house belonging to some of Mom(M)'s colleagues. Even though the water heater was out of order, my Brother(B) and I had gone in for a swim; our lips are purple, our skin wrinkled, and we're sitting on the edge of the pool wrapped in towels with colorful stripes.

There were a lot of supermarket receipts (almost all for hair dye and face creams), airline tickets (to San Francisco), birthday cards, wedding and baptism invitations (the children and grandchildren of certain writers and other well-known people) I had a separate pile for the landscapes and out-of-focus pictures, and added the ones with only feet, hands, or unrecognizable bits of heads, plus the large number of images of empty rooms and inanimate objects.

But the great treasure consisted of thirty or forty photographs from which Marisa(M_x) had cut out the subjects. You could see the scissor marks around "someone" who was apparently important. It wasn't out of spite; in fact she'd selected those she treasured most dearly. That much became clear later, in the study, when I saw the enormous collage on which all those absent characters coexisted. What wasn't clear to me was why she'd kept all those squares and rectangles with holes in them. The only thing still visible was the setting, from which the person in question was exiled, separated forever. Those characters would never return to their original contexts, and none of those "frames" now had any time. Didn't have the courage to throw out that small collection, so put it in my backpack and took it home.

Through them, you can see the world "from above"—that's why I like Venn diagrams. There isn't much documented evidence of this, but during the military dictatorship in Argentina, teaching basic set theory was prohibited in schools. We know, for example, that a tomato belongs to the tomato(TO) set and not to onions(ON) or chilies(CH) or coriander(CO). Where's the threat in reasoning like that? In set theory, tomatoes, onions, and chilies might realize they are different foodstuffs, but also that they have things in common, like the fact that they can all belong to the fresh hot salsa(FHS) set and, at the same time, to the Universe(U) of cultivated plants(CP), and might perhaps unite against some other set or Universe(U); for example, that of canned hot salsa(CAHS). In short, form a community of vegetables. Venn diagrams are tools of the logic of sets. And from the perspective of sets, dictatorship makes no sense, because its aim is, for the most part, dispersal: separation, scattering, disunity, disappearance. Maybe what worried them was that children would learn from an early age to form communities, to reflect collectively, to discover the contradictions of language, of the system. Visualized in this way, "from above," the world reveals relationships and functions that are not completely obvious.

Didn't see anything of Alonso(A) during the first months. Chema said he had things to do at the university in the United States where he was working on his PhD in literature, but would be back in the summer. He gave me a check to cover my fee until then. I deposited almost the whole sum into my savings account, keeping only what was needed for gas and daily expenses. The calendar didn't mean much to me, having neither a proper job nor vacations, but I understood we were going to meet in June and it was then the middle of April. Six months had gone by. Six months hoping for a repentant Tordo(T) to call, and those same six months trying to resign myself to the fact that this would never happen.

The landscape of time is pretty extensive. On the pine plywood boards, it wasn't just the time contained in the wood grain that was visible: there, in black, white, and grays, was everything I'd outlined and filled in with my brush. The third board remained unpainted. It made sense to do only two; together they were like an enormous double-leaf door, an entrance to another dimension (an entrance I still didn't know how to open).

If I were to throw a stone into a pond, it would cause tiny concentric waves to form in the water, and these would radiate out one by one until they disappeared. Diagrammatically, those waves also form a cone. The tip is the point and instant the stone hits the water, and the body is the waves opening out and spreading one by one. All this is important because time behaves in a very similar way to cones of light. I may be misinterpreting Stephen Hawking, but every event in the Universe(U)—just like the stone in the water—unfurls one cone of light toward the past (←) and another toward the future (→). The present, this exact moment, is where the tips of the two cones meet. The scientific diagram of time is a mirror image of a cone, a sort of hourglass. My particular case can only be described if two cones—Tordo(T) and Mom(M)—are located in the past, and their superimposed reflection, in the future. That is the only way to explain my feeling of being inside a washing machine on the rinse cycle, or why the future, from here, resembles the entrance to a whirlpool:

Marisa(M_x) Chubut was born ten years before Mom(M). She too was an exile from the Argentinian dictatorship. But her story was different from my parents'. My system for organizing everything that came out of her desk was simple. First, large groups: documents, newspaper clippings, manuscripts, recipes. Then a detailed classification of each batch. Told Chema I would need more stationery, and the following day had a box of a hundred green folders and another of pink ones. At that moment, Marisa(M_x)'s room became a city—the piles of papers were the buildings, and the streets were the spaces they enclosed. I liked being in that city. My time was divided between that parallel Universe(U^{II}), in which (I) coexisted with the absence of Marisa(M_x), and my original Universe(U), in which (I) coexisted with the absence of Mom(M). (I) moved from the perimeter of the bunker to the perimeter of that room on the top floor of a house in Tizapán, San Ángel (and vice versa).

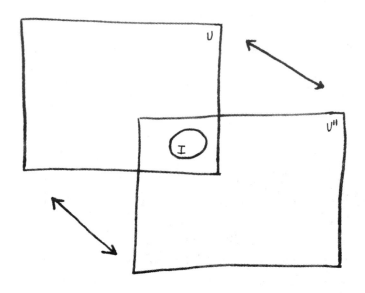

I have this nightmare: want to speak, but can't. Want to
cry out, but can't.

Inside each of the folders was a small story, green if it finished happily, pink if badly. Invitation to attend the wedding of Marisa(M_X) Chubut and Tono(T_N) García, Argentinian marriage certificate, and Mexican divorce certificate: a love story reduced to three pieces of paper inside a pink folder. Birth certificate (Argentina, 1973), certificate of baptism, elementary school grades (average, seven and a half), secondary school grades (average, seven and a half), barium enema results, and International Vaccination Certificate in a green folder, with a Post-it reading, "Alonso García Chubut/CASE HISTORY." Handwritten will of Mauricio Chubut (father of Marisa(M_X)) and photocopy of the family tree of the house of Chubut, copies of payments to Gonzalo Elizondo, letter to my dearest grandchildren (June 1, 1965), inventory of the estate, death certificate (automobile accident), all in a pink folder. This Post-it read, "Mauricio Chubut/GRANDFATHER."

Dendrochronology wasn't going to solve the mystery of time in the pine plywood boards. Tree rings give clues to environmental processes, but there were no books or articles on how to study the patterns of grain lines or their potential for disordering everything: breaking it into pieces, and then reuniting those pieces in a different form, or leaving them to drift. Almost all the specialized texts focus on climate change, and it was impossible to understand them fully. Must have stared at the treetops through the library window for many hours. Every so often I'd reread certain paragraphs in search of some possibly overlooked clue, but boredom usually won out, and I'd fall asleep with my head resting on the table until Violeta came by to collect me.

Alonso(A) had a sad expression, but he laughed at anything and everything. That made me feel insecure (or very stupid), because it wasn't really possible to ask him what the hell he thought was so funny. I'd get irritable, but still spent the day waiting for the moment when he'd finally decide to come up to Marisa(M_x)'s room to interrupt my silent routine with his awkward laugh. Afterwards, it occurred to me I could do or say certain things (very few) that made him nervous, and then his laugh sounded different. (I succeeded in deciphering the range of his tones of voice, breathing patterns, and volumes because that was the only way to know for sure what was happening to him or how he felt: if he was laughing because he was feeling fine, or bad, or nervous, or whatever.) At those moments, it seemed to me he was the one who was insecure, not me. A small victory. Alonso(A)'s presence made that parallel Universe(U^{II}) that (I) was gradually moving into more concrete:

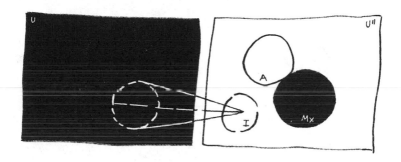

This morning a different sound woke me. Nuar ran around the whole apartment with her tail bristling, then hid behind the bookcase. It sounded as if something ceramic had fallen onto the kitchen floor and shattered.

Even though it was a matter of escape, of remaining for as long as possible in my parallel Universe(U^{11}), the other Universe(U) was still exerting its gravitational pull, and it finally sucked me back in: Jurgen(J) on the phone—his first and last call. Guessed our nocturnal encounters were about to end (and yes, he asked me not to come looking for him anymore) but didn't pay much attention to him because Alonso(A)'s face fell apart—almost sure it fell apart—and that was more important. The frontier separating the parallel Universe(U^{11}) and the Universe(U) disappeared with the ringing of a cell phone. Would like to be able to say everything was more mixed up than ever, but in fact, what was left was an implacable order that didn't bode well for me.

The newspaper clippings say she was a writer, that she died at the age of sixty-five and published only one book in her entire life. Although I'm no expert, something tells me it wasn't a great work of literature. She was also an actress, but she'd only given a single performance in Argentina and one dramatized poetry reading in Mexico. Despite the many newspaper clippings about her book and her excellent acting in that stage play, Marisa(M_x) Chubut was a secondary character. She was in the center of the "artistic world," but she was no one.

Probably felt a certain amount of empathy for her because I'd become a secondary character in my own life. In books, those sorts of insignificant beings attract me strongly: the ones who feel tiny, but are in fact enormous; the ones who seem gigantic, and are only inflated paper bags. But being incidental in real life is another story. A photograph of three personages, cut from the social pages in 1979, was particularly revealing; underneath, it said, in these exact words: "Josefina Vicens (left), Vicente Rojo (right), and unidentified

woman (center)." Unidentified woman. That was Marisa(M_x).
Someone who is no one.

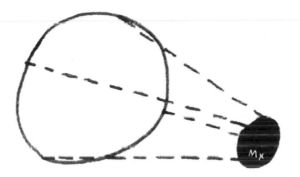

How are your telescope observations going? Alonso(A) asked after a period of silence.

Oh, bad news. I'm not cut out to be an astronomer. I've been looking at everything but the stars . . . But, hey, you haven't said if you want to come to Argentina . . .

He didn't reply.

How long since you've been there?

. . . Not since I was a child.

. . . Wouldn't you like to go back? I insisted.

Yeah, I would.

. . . With me?

Yeah, with you.

. . . So?

So what?

Shall we go?

. . . Sure, let's do it.

And at times we've thought Mom(M)'s story would have more meaning if we could go somewhere like the Plaza de Mayo to demand her return, to ask: Where is she? But that's absurd, because she didn't disappear like the others. Or did she? It's a logical absurdity because if it were possible for us to go to the Plaza de Mayo and demand her return, we would never have been born in the first place.

All her manuscripts were replicas of the same thing over and over. The only change was the writing, a firm hand becoming increasingly tremulous until it was practically illegible. What I discovered was not Jack Torrance's manuscript in *The Shining;* Marisa(M_x)'s were "clean" copy after "clean" copy of a handwritten book that never managed to get to its ending. That had no ending, no title, no date. That just ran out of words. I read the first sentence so many times I knew it by heart: "Impossible to return to the place one has left." It reminded me of the tangos Mom(M) used to listen to when she was feeling nostalgic.

Found *Exile*—Marisa(M_x)'s only publication—in the bookcase and compared it to the multiple manuscripts: this text did have an ending. Alonso(A) had suggested other unpublished works might turn up among her papers, but the copies I discovered weren't even corrected versions; each and every page said exactly the same thing, with the commas and periods in the same places. Don't know if it was her melodrama that made me indignant—"Mother!

Father! Will I ever see you again? Why have you left me so alone? Why have you abandoned me? Is not life now a form of death?"—or if it annoyed me to see myself reflected in such schmaltzy phrases: "I am a quiescent absence in the tragedy of my life" (the word *quiescent* is so pedantic). Was on the point of giving up, but morbid curiosity won out. While reading, I wondered if Alonso(A) had ever opened the book.

Marisa(M_x) began a single story many times, and that seems to me an admirable undertaking. Many different outsets can only be synonymous with many failures, with deformed narratives. That's what (I) have, a list of scattered fragments:

—A tangle of sets.
—Interchangeable subsets.
—Invisible intersections.
—Temporal inclusions.
—Sudden disjunctions.

Beginning the same text many times is, at the very least, an insistence on telling and understanding the same story.

In any other way, you fail time and again, beginning different stories that always end the same.

In any other way, you fail over and over, attempting to disorder time.

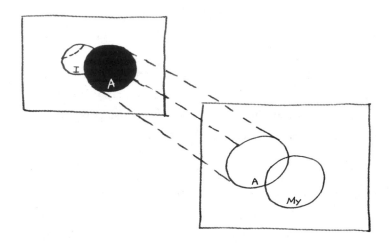

It's at the boundaries—on the edges—where things tend to blur.

My Brother(B) often used to tell Mom(M) his secrets. They'd chat for hours about things I wasn't supposed to know. For me, there was never a secret interesting enough to be confided to her. Don't think I have any real secrets. Well, just one. Would prefer not to have to keep it, but when I try to tell it, it can't be heard; it's infuriating, no one understands. I didn't choose that secret, we didn't choose it, it's here despite me, despite us. As a child, I used to wonder why my Brother(B) had so many secrets to tell, when none ever occurred to me. Or maybe it's a matter of being able to recognize them. How many would I need to have to be a normal person? That single secret came on the scene right when we stopped seeing Mom(M). It's a secret (I) share with my Brother(B), without even understanding it. A secret is like an invisible subset.

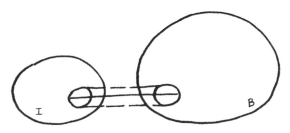

We run from the parking lot to the museum, but even so arrive drenched.

My sneakers are like paddling pools, says Alonso(A).

Yeah, it sounds funny when you're walking.

I'm still not used to these unpredictable D.F. rain-storms. I'll get a cold, or pneumonia or something . . . I look ridiculous, I'm not sure I should go in like this.

(Went through the door into the exhibition as if I hadn't heard those last words. We were already there.)

Don't you read the introductory wall text? he asks.

No, it's always incomprehensible. They should put it at the end.

And this *is* comprehensible?

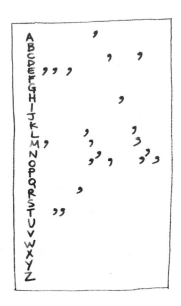

Hey. And so how do I look? Like a wet dog, I guess.

(He laughs out loud at everything I say, just for a change.)

You should hear your laugh. It's unsettling.

(He laughs again.)

Or better yet, indecipherable . . .

You look fine. You look . . . pretty.

(Swallowed, the saliva went down the wrong way, and I had a coughing fit—a disaster.)

Hey, the other day. That call, was it your . . . ?
Ah, he's German with a footballer's name . . .
And are you . . . ?
No, it's over.
. . . 'Cause?
His girlfriend's visiting.
Well . . .
Yeah, I know, it's not good . . .
Hmm? I didn't say anything . . . Do you speak German?
No.
Does he speak Spanish?
Don't think so. To be honest, we didn't speak much.
So?

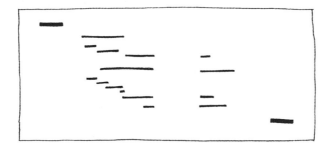

Well, what do you think? (Looking at the floor.)

Is this decipherable? (Trying to change the subject.)
Why do you want to know?
Well, because there could be a secret in it.
But if it's a secret, there's no sense in deciphering it.
You're a skeptic.

Maybe . . .
Do you have secrets?
Guess so.

Don't think I do. It'd be good to know what they're like. (He laughs.)

Guess you think I'm crazy.

No, not at all . . . I don't even want to imagine what you think of me!

That you're a skeptic, like I said, and that your laugh is a bit hostile but very attractive.

(Managed to leave him speechless.)

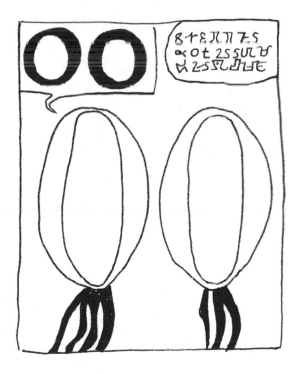

Would you tell anyone your secrets?

That's a really weird question.

Proposed we keep a secret neither of us understood (so it would never stop being a secret). He said he'd need to give it some thought.

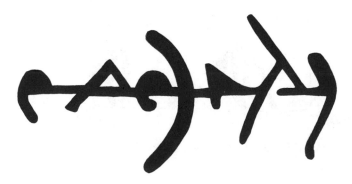

Took that as a yes.

(I) couldn't wait a second longer, so thought one up, disordered the syllables, and whispered it in Alonso(A)'s ear: (he gave a nervous little laugh).

When two people share a secret, they look more or less like this:

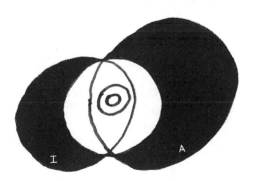

Who the hell is Nuar purring at?

With a little reconstruction here and a little there, I ended by understanding more about Marisa(M_X)'s exile than my own parents'. When she landed in Benito Juárez airport in March 1976, she was thirty-eight and had a three-year-old son. Her husband, Tono(T_N), didn't join them until almost a year later because it was much more difficult for him to get out. Marisa(M_X) had lived in Buenos Aires for just over half her life. She did several acting workshops (she met Tono(T_N) in one of them), and worked in a variety of government cultural offices to pay the rent.

At the beginning of 1976, Tono(T_N) directed a play ("original and experimental" according to the independent press of the day) called *Autopsy on an Outline* in which Marisa(M_X) played the female lead. It ran for only one night. When a number of the actors were disappeared the day after the premiere, Marisa(M_X) panicked, tried to change her and Alonso(A)'s names but couldn't. Then she used all her savings to buy two airline tickets to Mexico, and she and Tono(T_N) agreed they would meet up there. A friend had offered them her house in Cuautla.

In *Exile,* Marisa(M_X) gives a few details of the period before her involuntary expatriation but concentrates on a return trip she made to Argentina in 1984. It was just her and Alonso(A)—she'd gotten divorced by then. During that visit she decides to go back to the house in which she was born but discovers a larger building has taken its place. She also rings the doorbell of the big old house she once shared with Tono(T_N)—where she got pregnant, where they rehearsed from morning to night for months— but no one answers. She tries again the next day, and comments in her book: "The curtain of our bedroom window twitched, there was someone inside." But no one opens the door. Right there, at the entrance to what was once her home, she has a nervous breakdown and ends up in hospital. Those spaces she now needs to return to no longer exist, and that is the root of her tragedy: nothing belongs to her. Apparently, the consequences of dictatorship are felt afterwards, long afterwards. Exile is simply a way of delaying them. Sooner or later—SLURPPP—a strange force sucks you in, and there's no escape route. While narrating this episode, she scarcely mentions Alonso(A). Wonder just what he did at that moment; he was barely eleven.

After a couple of weeks, Marisa(M_X) leaves the hospital and buys the return tickets. She never again sets foot in Argentina. Upon her return to Mexico, she has herself voluntarily admitted to a psychiatric clinic. Wonder if Alonso(A) spent that time with Tono(T_N), if anyone explained to him what was going on. It's in the clinic, it seems, that she begins writing her memoir. Guess that's the cause of the obsessive repetitions and the tremulous hand of her manuscripts. It's not clear how long she stayed there, or the time that elapsed between one copy and the next. Wonder if exile converted her into a secondary character, or if she had always been one. Put the manuscripts into hypothetical (pretty pessimistic) chronological order: first those with the clearest writing, and then the ones in which the letters gradually become incomprehensible symbols. They didn't fall into the categories of either the pink or green folders, so I simply fastened them together with a binder clip.

I'm fond of the Main Library, a book building that seems to taper toward its summit, with an elevator that gets slower the more floors it ascends. It still feels like the same place I went to with Mom(M) as a kid: the crotchety unionized librarians, the eighties furnishings, and that very particular UNAM bustling hubbub of hundreds of people entering and leaving. There can't be a noisier library in the entire world. At elementary school, summer vacation started very early, and as Mom(M) had nowhere to leave me, she'd take me with her to her classes, a pack of felt-tip pens and an abstract art coloring book in my hand. We always made an obligatory stop in the library: I'd help her find a book, or we'd return ones she'd taken out. I liked reading the things she would later write on the board, although I naturally didn't understand a thing. Her classes were on psychoanalysis. I remember—because it was the only term that formed part of my childhood vocabulary—the word *Phantom* frequently appeared (like that, with a capital letter). When asked in school what my Mom(M) taught, I used to say phantoms. Everyone stared, open mouthed.

With the aim of extending my stay, I classified all the recipes Marisa(M_x) had cut from magazines and newspapers: breakfasts, starters, main courses, desserts, etc. Then put them in separate files.

I told Alonso(A) a lot of things about myself. Not about the bunker, or any of that stuff. Other sorts of things. It felt weird to hear my voice outside my head. Words frighten me. The idea of not knowing what others understand when you speak scares me. Alonso(A) told me things too. Not about Marisa(M_x)'s death or her crisis. But we did talk about Argentina: neither of us understands why a can of apricots in syrup with Chantilly cream (or worse still, caramelized milk) is the dessert of choice in that country.

Are you a painter or do you do weird stuff? he asks out of the blue.

Well . . . weird stuff, I guess.

Right. So are you one of those artists who doesn't know how to draw?

(It was probably a joke, but for me, not a particularly funny one.) Yeah, that's it. One of them . . .

I told him, for example, about my life drawing class at La Esmeralda. It was a simple exercise: copying the hand of the model. Up to that time, my drawings had been awful, and the teacher had no patience with me. But that day I really focused, wanting to do well. The more realistic the drawing, the better the grade. At the end of the class, the whole group gathered around each of the tables in turn to discuss the work. I'd made an effort, so felt calm, and though still among the worst in the class, this was by far my most proficient attempt of that semester. When we got to my table, the prof stood looking at my drawing for a long time, not saying a word. I thought he was finally going to leave me in peace, had nothing to say, or couldn't accept my improvement (because he hated me).

Better, Verónica. But why have you drawn a hand with six fingers?

Alonso(A) let out a laugh, identical to the one that had exploded through the whole of my class, and then he tried to make amends:

I can't draw either.

But there's no reason for you to be able to . . .

To compensate, he told me a story: in his preschool English class, he was asked to make a Halloween drawing. He painted a piece of white card completely black and took it to his teacher, who made a wry face and asked him what he'd drawn. He said it was night. Miss Ramírez rose from her chair, called for attention, and addressed the whole group: "Listen, children. None of you are going to give me anything like this, right?" I tried to stifle a giggle, but as

Alonso(A) always laughed at everything, there was really no need.

Have you still got the painting?

I threw it in the trash, outside the classroom.

Ugh, I'd love to have it.

He smiled. After that, it would never have even entered my mind to become an artist, he said, and then stood staring at my mouth . . .

Something was about to happen (the uncontrollable pangs in my pelvis were telling me so). I liked the way Alonso(A) understood night. We pretended the tension didn't exist.

But the phantoms are in the past. Or come from the past.
There are no phantoms here.

$$\frac{\text{DISAPPEARANCE}}{\text{APPEARANCE}} = \frac{\text{x}}{\text{PHANTOM}}$$

To find the secret word, the one we need, x has to be solved.

The bunker (or Mom($\mathbf{M}$)) is the unknown, x.

There are—I'm certain of this—things that can't be told in words.

I'll never know who S. is.

Try to organize Grandma(G)'s medicine chest. Most of the pills are past their expiration date. Everything has different names here. Sometimes it feels like, for her, taking medicines is just a routine, and she allows herself the pleasure of choosing them by their colors. The chest is so disorganized, it's a mystery to me how she ever manages to find anything. There's absolutely nothing for a sore throat, and swallowing is still painful. Decide to use Grandma(G)'s method and pick out two tablets at random—one pink, the other white—and put them into my mouth.

Sat down in front of the chest at the foot of the bed and opened it with a key I'd found in one of the desk drawers. There were a great many letters inside. Divided them up simply: "letters from Marisa(M_x) to" and "letters to Marisa(M_x) from." There were some—definitely love letters—Tono(T_N) had written her during a period he spent in Cuba at the beginning of the eighties, before their separation. There were also letters from the time of the dictatorship, which were succinct and few in number. They said very simple, sometimes absurd things. But there was more to it, something only those two understood, a personal language. Suppose that's love. Possibly shouldn't have read them, it wasn't part of my task, but Alonso(A) never asked for details. Don't know if he can even imagine just how many things are in the various pieces of furniture in his mother's room. At least now someone knows Marisa(M_x)'s story. Is there anyone who knows Mom(M)'s? If that person exists, I'd like to ask him or her a couple of questions.

It's your job to call Grandma and tell her we're coming.

But it was your idea to go . . . Why don't you . . . ?

Because I got in first, so you lose.

My Brother(B) is the first-born son; he's a historian but earns a living making documentary films. Sometimes he writes the scripts for them, sometimes he edits or directs them, and sometimes he does all three. He says he's become an expert on the microhistory of Mexico City and its surrounding areas. He's an expert on, for example, the abandoned railway station in Pantaco, the history of the Hotel Isabel, the construction of footbridges, the gutter press in D.F., and the Iztapalapa Passion Play.

OBSERVATION SHEET I

LOCATION:	Parque de las Américas, Colonia Narvarte.
DATE:	September 20, 2003.
LIGHT POLLUTION (1–10):	10.
OBJECT:	Woman and son.
SIZE:	Approximately thirty-seven and seven years of age.
CONSTELLATION:	Family.
LOCAL TIME:	11:30.

OBSERVATION:

NOTES:

Mother and son doing yoga on damp grass. Manage to make out that the boy is wearing a T-shirt with the yellow-on-black Batman logo. He squints when he's in the balancing poses. His "downward-facing dog" is a perfect triangle. They both have wet butts. Their bodies form letters, but the message is indecipherable.

Hungry? Yes. We were leaving the museum, and I suggested dinner. He said he couldn't, that he had to work on his thesis and get changed because he felt wrong in damp clothes. Then, in the car, I persuaded him to change his mind. Not sure how. There were crosswords printed on the restaurant tablecloths. While waiting for our food, we guessed at solutions. I found "to solidify or gel": *set*. Alonso(A) got "a word preceding 'headed'; silly or ignorant": *empty*.

Among the letters was, surprisingly, the manual for the telescope. It's the type of manual that's more complex and confusing than the thing you want to learn to use, but it has interesting diagrams, a sample **OBSERVATION SHEET**, and lots of symbols to help you make notes. For example, this is an orbit:

This signifies "planetary dark spots":

This, obviously, is infinity:

And this signifies uncertainty
(of course, it had to be a triangle):

Didn't say anything. Maybe just "aha." Nothing more. Alonso(A) knows that I know his girlfriend is in San Francisco. What I didn't know was if he knew I was going to miss him.

Wrote him an e-mail, but regretted it the moment I clicked Send:

August 13

Solona,
Tahw era uoy pu ot?
M'i ssingmi uoy llyfuaw . . .
V.

Luckily, his name appeared in my inbox five days later:

Dear Verónica,
I have decided to change my thesis topic. I'll
miss the old one. Wrote a paper on acrostics yesterday.
You can take the telescope if you want. There are
too many things in the house anyway.
A.

His mail initially seemed evasive, disappointing. Then I looked up the word *acrostic* in hopes of finding a clue. The dictionary says: "A verse or arrangement of words in which the initial letters or words in each line form a word or message." Reread his message vertically, like a detective who has finally discovered who the murderer is; my heart could have been heard beating on the other side of the city. Took his offer of the telescope literally.

Is there anything so simple and so devastating as a stupid coffee mug?

Ordering the correspondence chronologically was a way of taking up time, but could only be bothered to read a few of the letters from her sister Malena and other family members. At the bottom of the chest was a black bag with dozens of others that had been cut into small pieces. It felt like a treasure trove. They weren't written by Marisa(M_x). In fact, on comparing the handwriting with all the other letters, there was no match. Tipping the contents of the bag onto a rug reminded me of the Christmases when my Brother(B) and I—bored after so many days of vacation—would do jigsaw puzzles in the kitchen. There was undoubtedly some mystery behind those vestiges. Some of the fragments contained dates coinciding with Marisa(M_x)'s arrival in Mexico, although the handwriting was not, by any stretch of the imagination, Tono(T_N)'s. Then I separated out the scraps signed "S." That didn't tell me much either.

My only hope was to reconstruct them. As Alonso(A) wasn't around, there was no risk of him finding me out. I was, and knew it, returning the letters to a place where they no longer belonged; Marisa(M_x) must have had a purpose in hiding away that story in illegible disorder. And as the letters were gradually reassembled, my conscience became increasingly uneasy. I'd taken on the task of returning to a moment that no longer existed, to the moment when the things those letters said were still true.

Looked through all the photographs again in search of S., did the same with the clippings, but couldn't find him.

Things move around in the bunker. Or at least that's how it seems. Hadn't I left that book on the table, not on the desk? Or my shoes in the living room, not under my bed? Could have sworn I'd bought a yogurt, but there is none in the refrigerator. Perhaps my Brother(B) had come by and was responsible for the yogurt, but taking my shoes to the bedroom, never. My Grandma(G) says the same when I call to tell her we're coming to visit:

How are you, Grandma?

Someone keeps moving everything around, sweetie! I put something in one place, and it appears in another.

Are you sure?

Maybe it's absentmindedness or failing eyesight, but it's beginning to happen to me too. I'm not really surprised; there's not a single physical law that's respected in the bunker, apart from the law of chaos.

Two telegrams: the last messages from S. to Marisa(M_x).
Une dated late '76 and the other January '77. Tono(T_N) arrived in Mexico sometime in January or February '77.

It was an ending in two parts.

Both very brief.

Like everything that finishes.

This was the first:

12/31/76

Happy New Year STOP

S STOP

And the second was spine chilling:

01/31/77

I know I'll see you again STOP

Love confirms the circularity of the universe STOP

S STOP

The telescope manual also contained a small section on punctuation marks and letters used to describe weather conditions:

    (.) Precipitation reaching ground level.
    ,   Intermittent drizzle.
    ,,   Continuous drizzle.
    .   Light intermittent rain.
    :   Moderate intermittent rain.
    ;   Intermittent rain and drizzle.
    s   Dust suspended in the atmosphere.

Could that climatic symbology be used to read the piece made up of commas and letters we saw at the exhibition? It would indicate a sort of continuous and intermittent drizzle between the letters of the alphabet. That would be a deeply sad text.

I want to cook something special, says my Grandma(G).
But it's getting late, so maybe better to have a fried egg.
Mom(M) used to solve every problem with an egg too. The
crockery we're eating from is the same set we used when
your Mom(M) was a girl, she adds proudly. Grandma(G)
likes to reuse the yerba mate tea bags. She can't start the
day without a cup of mate; it's three in the afternoon, but
I don't say so. She forgets that the used bags are kept in
the refrigerator and takes out a new one each time. Your
Mom only ever ate her eggs hard boiled, she says. The
refrigerator is a cemetery of mate bags. She says I don't
tell her anything nowadays. Says that before, I used to tell
her everything (Before, when?), that I'm very reticent. My
throat is sore, but I don't say that either. Speaking is difficult. Attempt to stop hearing my thoughts, to reduce them
to the point that they seem incomprehensible.

We always realize things afterwards. Loneliness, for example. It's not when we think we're alone, or when we feel abandoned. That's something different. Loneliness is invisible, we go through it unconsciously, without knowing. At least that's true of the sort I'm talking about. It's a kind of empty set that installs itself in the body, in language, and makes us unintelligible. It appears unexpectedly when we look back, there in a moment we hadn't noticed before. I've probably never been so alone as when Mom(M) disappeared. There was no time to stop and think about it. I see myself sitting with my Brother(B) in the dining room, each of us with a sandwich of cheese and a smear of mustard on Bimbo bread, plastic cups of Coca-Cola, and it makes me sad. The two of us are acting as if those cups were made of glass. What else could we do? (I) realize how alone we were, both of us. How defenseless my Brother(B) and (I) were.

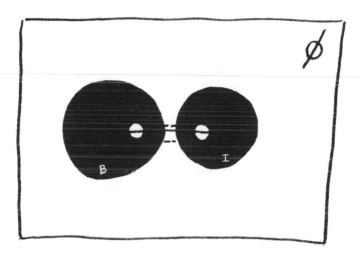

Then came the moment I had feared: there was no longer any pretext for continuing to go to Marisa(M_x)'s room. All that was left was to put everything into cardboard boxes, then label and close them. And there was no pretext for sending another e-mail to Alonso(A). He didn't write to me either. Don't know why, but spent my days waiting for him to return. Then wrote anyway.

September 5

Solona,
S'woh ruoy sisthe inggo? S'tahw ti bouta?
Tenlis, I nishedfi zingnigaor ruoy ther'smo chivear.
Tub won ev'I tog a blempro:
I kniht I ekil uoy. Stol.
V.

September 8

Dear Verónica,

Got to hand in a progress report on the thesis tomorrow.
The topic: essays "disguised" as novels. It's all the
same whether or not they accept it; just a formality. The
problem is I don't have much to say yet.

A.

If he liked me too, then the Universes(U, U^{II}) had finally
overlapped. And in the near future (I)'d be back in another
triangular map, but finally in the place (I) wanted to be, at
whatever cost.

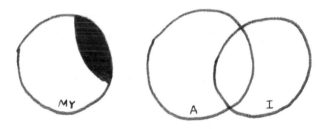

In my Grandma(G)'s head, today is thirty years ago.
  And it's also today.
  All at the same time.

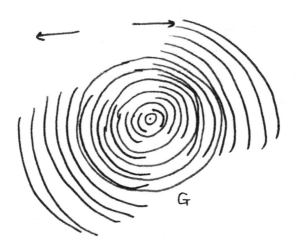

November 12, 1976

Marisa,

Putting dates on letters is a completely idiotic mania. What difference does it make at what moment in life everything overflows? And it's not as if I'm planning to publish them, the epistolary genre is too realistic. I'd prefer to find you lying in the sun beside the swimming pool in Cuautla.

I'll come to visit you soon. I love you.

S.

His letters were dazzling, exciting. It was as if he'd written them to me. But they were essentially impersonal, for effect only. Pure seduction. S. was writing to the future: he says that he won't publish his correspondence, so he probably will publish other things. Although the words might be addressed to Marisa(M_x), the message is a mirage. I can no longer remember what the letters I've written say. Is S. still alive? Seems like everything we write ends by being erased. That's as it should be. Nothing Marisa(M_x) and S. wrote to each other is true now. Were they in fact ready to change their lives to be together? What damn use are the vestiges of something that no longer exists?

Nuar has been sleeping on Mom(M)'s bed every night since I left the door open. Look in and whisper a request for her to come in with me, because the noises inside the bunker in the early hours are scary, but she takes no notice. Who knows why she prefers to sleep there? But every morning she puts her paw on my face to wake me, and I have to hide under the pillow if I want to go on sleeping.

September 24

Solona!
Eryev ningmor ni ym roombed uoy nac raeh: *bang,
bang, bang, bang* (eht borsneigh era ingdo pairsre
stairsup). Taht edam em kniht bouta "sesguidis." *Bang*
si a drow thoutwi a guisedis, t'nis ti?

Dna neht I soal thguoht pu a tsil fo sdrow htiw sesguidis: *aplomb, happenstance, disgruntled, quintessence,
halcyon, unquiet, jape, earthfall* . . . ereht era erom, tub
I deppots ereht.
V.

September 24

Dear Verónica,
Ha-ha. I use those words all the time!
You mean onomatopoeia, I think.
Are you serious about the disguise thing?
Crazy, but it has potential.
A.

Called Dad. Wanted to ask him if he has any idea what happened to Mom(**M**)—after all, he lived with her for twenty years—but didn't know how.

OBSERVATION SHEET V

LOCATION:	Parque de las Américas, Colonia Narvarte.
DATE:	October 13, 2003.
LIGHT POLLUTION (1–10):	10.
OBJECT:	Tree(top)s.
SIZE:	Circumference from 2 to 6 feet.
LOCAL TIME:	09:00.
EQUIPMENT:	None.

OBSERVATION:

NOTES:

Have been looking for a tree I carved my name on sometime in my childhood. Not sure which has disappeared, the carving or the tree. Or both?

Trees don't move around, but it's very difficult to find them.

Argentina. Sometimes see myself ringing Grandma(G)'s bell, and Mom(M) opens the door, as if she's been there all the time. The two women playing hide-and-seek in a small house in the Iponá neighborhood of Córdoba.

October 6

Ym raed Solona,
Si siht eht nninggibe fo thingsome?
V.

October 7

Dear Verónica,
If
we
don't
think
about
the
beginning,
there
will
never
be
an
end.
A.

Decided to call her Nuar. I hadn't had a cat since childhood and had forgotten how much you can enjoy their company. Nuar is mute. It took a while for me to realize that. One day, she came to where I was painting and tried to meow; she opened her jaws wide, but all that came out was a kind of muffled sound, a sort of barely audible purr she spat out from her stomach. Followed her into the kitchen, and she indicated that her saucer of water had tipped over. Nuar would spend hours sitting at the window looking out over the park where she was born; she also liked walking on the cornices and lying in the sun on the balcony. Some nights tomcats came to visit, and they'd talk to her from the side-walk or the park. Nuar would answer, but then immediately look to me, because they couldn't hear her. Some adventurous spirit once climbed a tree and got very close. Nuar stood stock-still, then made that muffled sound. The cat backed away and disappeared. It was as if she were talking in another tongue, not the one cats speak.

Was lucky enough to get a seat for Alonso(A) on the same flight.

Gave him his booking confirmation. He smiled.

He promised to return to D.F. in time for the trip. Before leaving, he asked:

Which do you prefer, the window seat or the aisle?

Aisle.

Great. I prefer the window.

He winked, stroked my neck, kissed me on the cheek, and left. Called him several times to say good-bye before he boarded the plane, but his phone was already switched off.

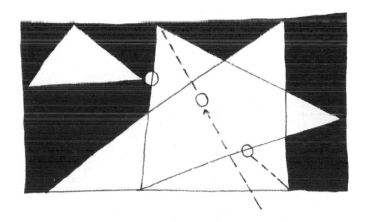

OBSERVATION SHEET IV

LOCATION:	Parque de las Américas, Colonia Narvarte.
DATE:	October 1, 2003.
LIGHT POLLUTION (1–10):	10.
OBJECT:	Truck.
SIZE:	40 feet.
MAGNITUDE:	Enormous.
CONSTELLATION:	Blockage.
LOCAL TIME:	10:00.
EQUIPMENT:	None.

OBSERVATION:

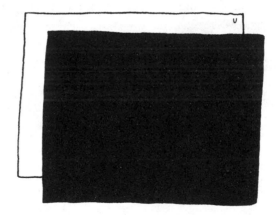

NOTES:

It's outside the park, blocking the view. A man sleeps in the driver's cab; he goes away in the mornings. Told myself I'd take the telescope up to the roof at night, but it's always too cloudy. Tried, but couldn't see anything. Should maybe find something else to do.

A Brief History of Time was by far the best thing I read during those days, not just because my research into time in tree rings had been a complete failure, but also because the book was fundamental to a better understanding of the bunker (said my Brother(B)). One day, when he dropped by to visit, I informed him that if a star dies, its last glimmer could take eight thousand million years to reach us.

Everyone knows that, Vero.

So didn't tell him the mind-blowing thing is that, apparently, the past doesn't disappear, it's still floating out there somewhere, and is constantly reconfiguring itself. It isn't necessarily what's in our memories. And so neither is time that linear concept we all think about; everything is topsy-turvy. What's strange is that scientists can investigate a past as remote as the origin of the Universe(U), but things here on planet Earth don't go backwards. For going back in time, all we have are telescopes and books, and maybe also trees. There's no other way of returning, even if it might sometimes seem we regress to the beginning, that life spits us out in front of the terrifying third-grade teacher.

October 7, 1976

Marisa,

I'd like to put the sky or the sea or the night into this letter. I'm writing just a few lines to propose we meet on October 29. Would that be all right? You set the time and place. If you're in Cuautla, it's no problem; I can go there. We could meet, even for a moment, in some park, at a church, or wherever you want. I promise not to distract you for too long. Don't worry, no one has noticed yet. Answer soon, time is short.

XX.

S.

This is the first letter from S. I reassembled. It was written on blue paper, so it was easy to identify the pieces and fit them together.

In his spare time, my Brother(B) has been working on another documentary. He says he's just playing, experimenting. He's become obsessed with high contrast, the way an image loses definition and becomes abstract when converted into just two tones. He does trial runs with reframed clips from documentaries he's already worked on. The close-up makes the images unrecognizable. Just blobs. He hasn't shown any of this to anyone. Not even me. There's no hurry, he says. Sometimes he tells me these things. He also says he's writing the script; it's going to have a voice-over offering reflections on geography. He wants to describe those high contrasts as if they were found maps, cities of pixels, islands of bits hiding in the memories of computers.

October 22

Dear Verónica,
I'm feeling this enormous urge to eat green pozole.
In the United States there's no green pozole; and in
Mexico there's no General Tso's chicken, which I love.
A.

Finally!

When (I) got to his house
Alonso(A) was stretched out on the sofa
watching a movie

swore not to remember which
because it was crap

it was such an anticlimax that my memory retained a
perfect image of the two of us sitting side by side
deadpan

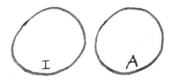

we turned

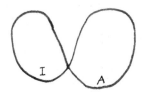

moved closer

he kissed my neck

felt his breath

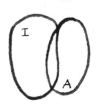

got goose bumps   giggled

bit his neck

he giggled too

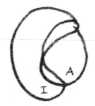

tangled up together

fell off the sofa

the floor was very cold

brrrrrrrrrrrrrrrrrrrrrrrrrr

(I) screamed

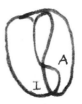

sprang up

ran to the bedroom

his eyes above mine
his weight resting on me

his eyes above mine
his weight

transfixes me

both
close our eyes
just for a second

time stops existing

Tordo(T) thought pool was a minor game, so he taught me billiards, which to him seemed a refined, almost artistic act. The shot that sends the balls careering randomly toward pockets is too elemental, he says derisively. I can almost hear his voice. In billiards you have to make the ball trace out a triangular figure inside a rectangle (the table). If the figure is perfect, it manages to hit other balls. One ball hits two others during the same trajectory. A game of three cushions. Pure mathematical coincidence. This is the infrathin, he concludes. Billiards was the second sign something was wrong . . . and I didn't see that one either.

He wasn't there. Not in the departure lounge, not at the boarding gate, not next to the window.

Alonso(A) wasn't there.

Didn't cry. Wanted to, but couldn't.

Just felt the urge to throw up.

His was the only empty seat on the plane.

Terribly cold because the cabin crew never brought me a blanket.

DAY ONE: Arrival in El Calafate. Those of us on the tour are the only guests in a gigantic hotel. The guide said the Perito Moreno glacier, which we are on, forms part of the Southern Patagonian Ice Field and extends for over ten thousand miles. Couldn't help but wonder if there were also disappeared persons under those enormous sheets of ice, and if one day global warming would finally bring them to light.

DAY TWO: Upsala & Onelli. More glaciers. The guide was inspired, she talked about the "ice witnesses." Cylindrical core samples several kilometers long (obtained by drilling into the glacier), in which the different layers of snow that have accumulated during each season are visible. It's a way of doing archaeology with ice. Wanted to ask her if it was like what happens with tree rings, but my tonsils were badly swollen.

DAY THREE: Ushuaia. From the plane, the Patagonian ice looks like a bluish desert: dunes of frozen water. We get to

Ushuaia in the late afternoon. There's a really damp cold that seeps through to my bones. Think I must have been running a fever all night: woke up in a sweat.

DAY FOUR: Left the group (didn't go to Tierra del Fuego National Park) to find an internet café.

Not a single e-mail from Alonso(A). Life's a bitch.

The city has a weird, almost ridiculously Dutch feel to it. Went into a restaurant and ordered Mom(M)'s favorite: a submarine (a bar of chocolate dunked in a mug of scalding hot milk). Then back to the hotel and to bed for the rest of the day.

DAY FIVE: End of the world. The guide commiserated with me and offered to take me to a pharmacy: it was closed. Before we boarded the ship, she pointed out a sign near the shoreline that read: USHUAIA. END OF THE WORLD. Everyone else took turns photographing one another. Wasn't in the mood, but offered my services as a photographer.

For some reason, thought that on crossing that limit, I'd understand something. But it turns out that the famous Lighthouse at the End of the World isn't the Lighthouse at the End of the World at all: the ship in fact takes you to the Les Eclaireurs (Explorers) Lighthouse, which is much closer, and you don't discover it's Explorers Lighthouse until you're there, beside a small island. The name of the real Lighthouse at the End of the World is the San Juan de Salvamento Lighthouse, and no tourist ship goes there because the facilities are used by the Argentinian Naval Hydrographic Service. *The Lighthouse at the End of the World* is in fact the title of a novel by Jules Verne, says the guide. It doesn't exist. The nerve! The most pathetic thing is that the ship does a U-turn at the supposed end of the world and sets off back, as if nothing had happened:

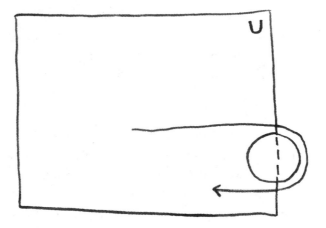

I was thinking "The End" might be a life jacket; wanted to drop anchor there. But one way or another, things succeed in returning to the outset, to some beginning.

Find our photo album on the table in the den. Sometimes think if an object in the bunker moves around, it's because it wants to tell me something. Sit down to look through the album, even though I know exactly what's in it and have already searched it for clues millions of times. But now, on the last pages, there are images that weren't there before . . . It dawns on me that they're the collection of "frames" I brought from Marisa(M_x)'s room. Not interested in knowing how they got there, but do want to decipher the message, otherwise, one day I'll end up like that: a hole cut out from some place.

It's a weird feeling to arrive at a place that corresponds to you, but where you don't belong. To recognize a street you didn't grow up on. Sleep, eat, take a shower in a house that should be just around the corner from your own. Wander through a neighborhood you didn't play in. Chat with people you never knew. Find a space just your size, but be unable to fill it. My Brother(B) had flown directly to Córdoba earlier that day. Grandma(G)'s house hasn't changed at all, he warned me as he let me in. Everything is older, that's for sure, including her. Everything is covered in dust.

The resemblance to the bunker is terrifying, he goes on to say while I'm unpacking. It's a sort of Southern Cone branch office, he insists.

On the bathroom walls, there are spiders and colonies of ants stuck in the cement: the walls were never tiled. On one side of the dining room is the gigantic cardboard box that once contained a new washing machine (bought the last time we were here) and is now used as a receptacle for redundant objects. Anything that doesn't work, or she can't decide where else to put, goes in the box. There are yellow-ish damp stains on all the walls. The soles of your shoes stick on the cheap vinyl floor tiles. An old refrigerator in the carport has been made into an archive for all my grandpa's papers. He died unexpectedly when I was twelve. Mom(M) didn't arrive in time to say good-bye; she didn't even see him before the burial. Everything smells of ammonia because of the cat pee; there are three felines living in the house: Mishima, Perlita, and Alelí. And another seven or eight come and go; they never enter the house, but there's always food left for them in the yard. Grandma(G)'s house is definitively unfinished, like my whole life.

December 30

Solona,
Eht houselight ta eht dne fo eht dlrow si a noc . . .
V.

My Grandma(G) is a hypochondriac and forgetful. We sleep together. Her bed creaks. She goes to the bathroom several times during the night. Whenever she stands up or snores— very loudly—it feels as if the wooden bed base has been holed and is going under. She also takes a siesta. Her siestas are getting longer and longer. In fact, she sleeps the whole time. It occurs to me that if she does this for ten seconds longer every day, she soon won't wake at all. I can't sleep if the sun is shining outside, it terrifies me. My Brother(B) is in what was Mom(M)'s bedroom. He says it's impossible to sleep on her mattress, you just sink like a ship. When she is awake, Grandma(G) goes around and around in circles. The hours slip away without her realizing. It gets too late for her knitting class, so she stays home. It gets too late for her to have her hair dyed, and she leaves it for another time. She's not letting herself go, says my Brother(B), it's a form of evasion. And all the other words associated with it: *avoid, escape, desert . . . elude . . . flee, sneak away, vanish . . . Disappear,* I say the word in the hoarse voice that's still unrecognizable to me. Disappear, echoes my Brother(B).

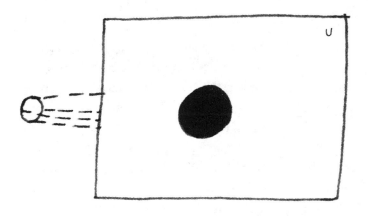

U

"Dust suspended in the atmosphere." That's what the telescope manual says *s* signifies. Don't believe S. was thinking of that when he chose his pseudonym, but even so he vanished into thin air.

We used to fry four eggs, Grandma(G) says, finally getting
back to the subject. Two for me and two for your grandpa.
Your mom liked hers hard boiled. Half a dozen eggs at
every breakfast. But I got them from a neighbor who kept
hens in her yard and sold them at a fair price. Nowadays,
you have to go to the supermarket for everything, no one
keeps hens in the yard anymore. I go to a convenience
store, just on the corner, there are huge supermarkets that
are good for shopping because the prices are lower, but I
don't have transportation, and cabs are very expensive, so
I just go to the place nearby; now they've gone and changed
the boy who works there, and the new assistant doesn't
make much of an effort . . . Grandma(G) pours pints of
Chuker into her yerba mate tea as she tells me this. Chuker
is a brand of liquid sweetener that tastes awful.

Another nightmare: Alonso(A) sends me an e-mail. Can't read it. It's written in a cowardly, indecipherable language. Wake trying to remember the words, but they no longer matter.

The trees in Grandpa's garden are withered. We used to have peaches and plums when we came to visit. At dinnertime, I'd go out to pick up a lemon or two from the ground to squeeze onto the salad. I only went to my grandpa's grave once. The lightbulb in the kitchen flickers—it drives my Brother(B) crazy—but no one does anything about it. The gravestone is laid flat against the ground. The remote for the television didn't have any batteries the last time we were here either. We've thought about buying some, but • still haven't gotten around to it . . . The gravestone has a small plaque with his name, and at one side there's a little hole for flowers. When did we last come to Argentina? In 1993, my Brother(B) says. And what year is it now? 2003.

(I) think up a plan for escaping unharmed from this story:

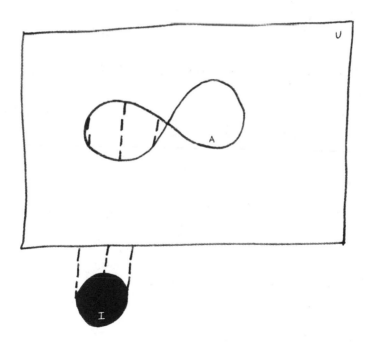

She's the image of Coty! cluck my Grandma(G)'s friends at the neighborhood cultural center. Grandma(G) managed to get ready in time, so the three of us went to a regional dance performance. Coty is my Mom(M). It's pronounced with the accent on the *y*. I've never asked why they call her that, and don't know if they're aware it's a brand of perfume. In their eyes, I'm a substitute for my Mom(M). It wasn't me they were seeing, but Coty, even my Grandma(G). A bunch of people for whom filling holes is enough. They all see Grandpa in my Brother(B) too. There's a sort of temporal superimposition going on. We are the past. They haven't changed. And perfumes tend to evaporate. It seems to me all of us have more than one role in life. (I) can recognize myself in several but can't manage to get the part (I) want.

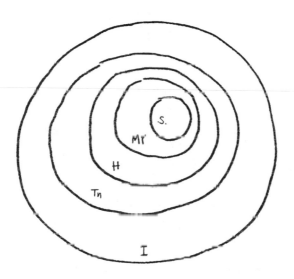

Was looking through Marisa(M_x)'s telescope. It was in the bathroom, and the space was cramped, but Alonso(A) came in to take a turn at the eyepiece anyway. Then he just stood there looking incredulous. Guess he thought it weird that the telescope was pointing at the cracks and stains on the opposite wall, but it seemed to me his mother must have had some reason for leaving it there, and I wanted to discover what that reason was. That was our first meeting.

As a child, I said, I wanted to be an astronaut, or at least an astronomer, but ended up studying visual arts because I don't understand the first thing about physics. Didn't you end up studying something really different from what you dreamed of doing when you were a little boy?

And there I came to a grinding halt.

How could I have used those words to introduce myself? No idea.

I eventually gave a shrug, disappointed, because my question was clearly inappropriate. Ought to have started with something like, "Hi, I'm Verónica." Although since he was the one to suddenly appear in the bathroom, it should have been up to him to begin with "Hi, I'm Alonso. Are you Verónica?" But then he would have looked silly, because it was obvious he was himself, and the person perched on the edge of the tub, looking through the telescope, was me.

But the bunker was at its weirdest when everything was calm. The absolute silence was often the forerunner of catastrophe.

The staircase Grandpa built in the living room doesn't go anywhere. You can't even use it because Grandma(G) put a bulky piece of furniture at the bottom, so as not to waste space. A shiver runs down my spine whenever I pass it. There was meant to be a second floor above. My Brother(B) and I should have lived upstairs, not around the corner. But Mom(M) left. Grandma(G) says my grandpa tried, unsuccessfully, to stop her; Mom(M) and Dad boarded a plane on March 24, 1976. We never lived in that house they never finished building, to which they never added a second floor. Never, never, never. Three times never. But they did build a staircase to the end of the world.

What's a Tordo?

An urban bird that looks like a rat, but with wings.

And why do they call you that?

. . .

Aren't you going to tell me?

It's stupid . . .

Hey, do you know anyone whose nickname isn't stupid?

Well . . . it's because I've had "speckled" hair since I was twelve.

Like it is now?

It's more even now, gray streaks. Before it was black and white, and it looked weird.

You were a gray-haired boy! Is that why you don't have any photos of when you were little?

I've got a few.

Are you going to show me them someday?

At the foot of my bed, a ball of rusty wire appeared, with a trail of earth leading to the window. Guessed Nuar must have found it in the tree by the cornice. The next day she left me a piece of red cloth smeared with automobile grease. No idea how to decipher these clues. The third day, it was a broken rubber band. The fourth, a dry twig. The fifth, the wing of a black butterfly. The sixth, nothing. The seventh, a dead bird.

Grandma(G)'s house is suspended in time. It's also stuck in the moment my grandparents last saw Mom(M). The house in Iponá and the bunker: a pair of found mirrors. The reflection becomes infinite. And the infinite is an eternally empty set.

How do you unmake a secret?

December 31

Solona,
Evol
firmscon
eht
tyrilacucir
fo
eht
verseniu,
V.

OBSERVATION SHEET II

LOCATION:	Not given.
DATE:	January 10, 2004.
LIGHT POLLUTION (1–10):	0.
OBJECT:	Not given.
SIZE:	Not given.
LOCAL TIME:	23:00.
EQUIPMENT:	Telescope.

OBSERVATION:

NOTES:

The above observation shows a neutrino: a type of subatomic particle with no charge, only half-integer spin, and a mass less than that of an electron. Neutrinos pass through matter without affecting it. In other words, they're phantom particles.

There was no answer. Rang the bell again. Several times, in fact. Thought I glimpsed a shadow behind the curtain, but no one opened up. Two hours sitting at the door. Zilch. Returned the following day: a sign was hanging in the window of Alonso(A)'s bedroom: FOR SALE.

Maybe Mom(M) is an ice witness.
Or a tree.
Trees don't move around.

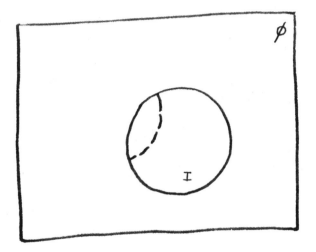

Argentina is once again very far away.

No sooner have we put the suitcases down in the entrance to the bunker than we hear noises in the kitchen.

In unison, my Brother(B) and I emit a loud "huh."

I peek around the door, motion for him to come and see.

We stare at each other.

Accomplices.

Skeptics.

It's the sound of the dustpan and broom.

Mom(M)?

She's sweeping up a broken coffee mug.

On one piece you can see the word:

STILL

The rest of the fragments are illegible.

And if it doesn't begin, and doesn't end, then what?

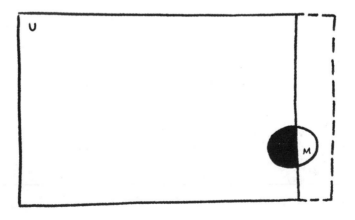

January 13

Ym rcstdca Solona,
Bang!
V.

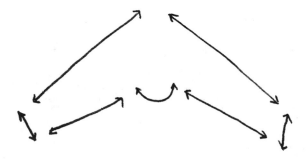

AFTERWORD: E-MAIL SET

The "E-mail Set" began its life as an electronic conversation related to a personal pronoun, and involved myself, Verónica Gerber Bicecci, and our editor at Coffee House Press, Lizzie Davis. It ran from January 2016 to April 2017.

The *I* problem:

In Spanish, it is possible to omit the personal pronoun, as it is indicated by the verb ending (for example, the *o* at the end of *escribo* [I write]). This grammatical peculiarity must be kept in mind when translating into English, since the translator will usually wish to avoid the repetitiveness of strings of sentences beginning with the same subject pronoun. The challenge is intensified in a text written in the first person. A further layer of complexity in *Empty Set* is that characters who are included in the Venn diagrams are indicated in the text by, as Verónica terms it, "gluing their letter to their name": Hermano(H) / Brother(B). So what to do with *I* immediately became a "thorny issue."

When I asked Verónica about her criteria for including or omitting the subject pronoun Yo(Y), she replied, "the designation of the letters points out—I believe—their role in the passages, as well as their place in the diagrams . . . I did try to consciously avoid an overpopulation of *Yo*, and used it only when I felt it was needed, or impossible to avoid in the structure of a phrase."

My quandary was, therefore, whether to "overpopulate" the text with I(I)s, not present in the original, or find another way of expressing the pronoun. One initial solution was to avoid it in English wherever possible. The obvious strategy was to use impersonal structures and the passive voice when appropriate, but I also simply omitted the pronoun when I felt the text was comprehensible and coherent without it. Although Ernest Vincent Wright managed to compose *Gadsby* without using the letter *e*, there seemed to be no way of erasing *I* from the translation of a first-person narrative into English without adding levels of complexity not present in the source text.

My possible solutions to the problem of how to express the unavoidable *I* eventually boiled down to:

1. Leave it as a normal *I* when not referring to a drawing.
2. Put it in brackets: (I).
3. Use the lowercase: i (maybe with capitals at the beginning of a sentence).
4. Use empty brackets to represent *I*: ( ).

Of these four choices, I initially liked the empty brackets, as it felt to me they "mirror the way *Yo* is absent but implicit in Spanish." The next stage was to produce four versions of the first pages of the text, which I then sent to Verónica and Lizzie.

Verónica gave three reasons for agreeing with my initial preference:

1. It's a conceptual decision that works perfectly well with the whole sense of the book.
2. It's an aesthetic risk that says a lot about the ideas inside the book, and I like these kinds of risks.

And finally but most importantly:

3. It's a very good way to make clear from the structure of the writing that this is another *Empty Set*, the one you're

writing and of which I'm just a reader, or cowriter. It's a way in which, I feel—but correct me if I'm wrong—you're able to appropriate the book in your own writing and reading. And this is exactly what we have to do, I think. So, in any case, I would really like us to choose every time in a way it can be more your book than mine.

Lizzie came back to us with a different response, one that encouraged us to view the situation from another angle:

I was thinking a lot about the bracketed initials while reading as well, and I'm glad you brought them up—it's a complicated issue. I think the trouble with modifying the personal pronoun each time it appears in the

English is the repeated interruption in the text that comes about as a result, a level of interruption that is not there in the original, and I worry that could be a bit distracting for a reader. We were thinking, too, that the more frequently the bracketed initials appear, the less potent they'll be in instances where they really were there in the Spanish—they may sort of lose their rarity and their punch. (And I'm sure you are thinking the same thing as you try to reduce the number of *I*s!) So, what do you think about leaving the *I*s as they'd normally appear in English, but using an (I) for the instances where Verónica uses Yo(Y)? I think that could help maintain the level of emphasis that's there in the Spanish while still allowing the (I) to function with the diagrams and carry the symbolic implications that go along with that when the author intended as much . . .

Both Verónica and I could see Lizzie's point about reducing the interruption into the text. From my viewpoint:

The implicit *Yo* in the Spanish is in fact active—she paints the plywood boards, she organizes Marisa's stuff, her grandmother's medicine chest, etc. Yo(Y) usually appears when the narrator is describing her position within the various sets and relationship to other sets. So the absence of the *I* in I(I) somehow reflects that it is the *I* in the diagram that is being referred to.

Verónica's response was: "I understand what you say: if she is 'inside' the brackets, then she is 'inside' the drawings by using just (I). I like it!"

However, there was no essential correspondence between the occurrence of Yo(Y) in the source text and the occasions when it would be necessary to include *I* in the English-language version, so the next step in my process involved where (I) should in fact appear:

> I've been thinking about only using it in sections that have an image containing Yo(Y): the only problem with this is that all the other characters/things referred to in the diagrams are bracketed whenever they appear, and it feels a bit too much to do the same with them . . . So maybe best only use (I) when referring to the drawings. What do you think?

Verónica then suggested only using (I) in paragraphs immediately preceding drawings, and my final decision was whether to use it only once, or throughout the preceding paragraph.

Problem solved!

As I read, reread, and refined the translation, progressively removing the first-person pronoun, a slight change in the rhythm of the English-language text occurred, one that I felt to be quite natural. I also had the sense that I was going through a mirrored refraction of Verónica's own creative conceptual process, and also, to some extent, taking the risky path she herself favored. This sense became so strong that I asked Verónica if she could produce images that would work with this afterword in a way that parallels their use in the main text.

This whole conversation, involving three voices with overlapping subjectivities and individual concerns, sums up for me what translation is about, and I hope this note offers readers an insight into the wider dialogue involved in the production of literary works in translation.

Christina MacSweeney
Norwich, April 2017
Artwork: Verónica Gerber Bicecci

AUTHOR'S ACKNOWLEDGMENTS

Infinite thanks to the Premio Aura Estrada and to Francisco Goldman. To the Ucross Foundation; the Ex Hacienda de Guadalupe, Oaxaca; and Ledig House for providing me with the space and time to write. To Guillermo Espinosa Estrada, Juan Pablo Anaya, Luis Carlos Hurtado, Elisa Navarro Chinchilla, José Aurelio Vargas, and Néstor García Canclini for reading and commenting on the many Spanish drafts, and, of course, to Christina MacSweeney for the original English-language manuscript of this work.

Part of the book was written with a grant from FONCA's Jóvenes Creadores program (first period, 2012–2013), under the tutorship of Jorge F. Hernández.

A number of the drawings are in homage to: Cy Twombly (page 39), Ulises Carrión (page 105), Alighiero Boetti (page 106), Jacques Calonne (page 107), Marcel Broodthaers (page 107), Carlfriedrich Claus (page 108), Mirtha Dermisache (page 108), Roberto Altmann (page 109), Clemente Padín (page 110), Vicente Rojo (page 110), and Carlos Amorales (page 111). Many thanks to them all.

TRANSLATOR'S ACKNOWLEDGMENT

I would like to thank Verónica Gerber Bicecci not only for the many insights she gave me into her text, but also for the friendship and hospitality she and her partner, Guillermo Espinosa Estrada, offered me during two trips to Mexico City, which coincided with the translation of *Empty Set*.

LITERATURE
is not the same thing as
PUBLISHINC

Coffee House Press began as a small letterpress operation in 1972 and has grown into an internationally renowned nonprofit publisher of literary fiction, essay, poetry, and other work that doesn't fit neatly into genre categories.

Coffee House is both a publisher and an arts organization. Through our *Books in Action* program and publications, we've become interdisciplinary collaborators and incubators for new work and audience experiences. Our vision for the future is one where a publisher is a catalyst and connector.

FUNDER ACKNOWLEDGMENTS

Coffee House Press is an internationally renowned independent book publisher and arts nonprofit based in Minneapolis, MN; through its literary publications and *Books in Action* program, Coffee House acts as a catalyst and connector—between authors and readers, ideas and resources, creativity and community, inspiration and action.

Coffee House Press books are made possible through the generous support of grants and donations from corporations, state and federal grant programs, family foundations, and the many individuals who believe in the transformational power of literature. This activity is made possible by the voters of Minnesota through a Minnesota State Arts Board Operating Support grant, thanks to the legislative appropriation from the arts and cultural heritage fund. Coffee House also receives major operating support from the Amazon Literary Partnership, the Jerome Foundation, The McKnight Foundation, Target Foundation, and the National Endowment for the Arts (NEA). To find out more about how NEA grants impact individuals and communities, visit www.arts.gov.

Coffee House Press receives additional support from the Elmer L. & Eleanor J. Andersen Foundation; the David & Mary Anderson Family Foundation; the Buuck Family Foundation; Fredrikson & Byron, P.A.; Dorsey & Whitney LLP; the Fringe Foundation; Kenneth Koch Literary Estate; the Knight Foundation; the Rehael Fund of the Minneapolis Foundation; the Matching Grant Program Fund of the Minneapolis Foundation; Mr. Pancks' Fund in memory of Graham Kimpton; the Schwab Charitable Fund; Schwegman, Lundberg & Woessner, P.A.; the U.S. Bank Foundation; VSA Minnesota for the Metropolitan Regional Arts Council; and the Woessner Freeman Family Foundation in honor of Allan Kornblum.

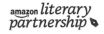

THE PUBLISHER'S CIRCLE OF COFFEE HOUSE PRESS

Publisher's Circle members make significant contributions to Coffee House Press's annual giving campaign. Understanding that a strong financial base is necessary for the press to meet the challenges and opportunities that arise each year, this group plays a crucial part in the success of Coffee House's mission.

Recent Publisher's Circle members include many anonymous donors, Suzanne Allen, Patricia A. Beithon, the E. Thomas Binger & Rebecca Rand Fund of the Minneapolis Foundation, Robert & Gail Buuck, Claire Casey, Louise Copeland, Jane Dalrymple-Hollo, Mary Ebert & Paul Stembler, Kaywin Feldman & Jim Lutz, Chris Fischbach & Katie Dublinski, Sally French, Jocelyn Hale & Glenn Miller, the Rehael Fund-Roger Hale/Nor Hall of the Minneapolis Foundation, Randy Hartten & Ron Lotz, Dylan Hicks & Nina Hale, William Hardacker, Jeffrey Hom, Carl & Heidi Horsch, Amy L. Hubbard & Geoffrey J. Kehoe Fund, Kenneth Kahn & Susan Dicker, Stephen & Isabel Keating, Kenneth Koch Literary Estate, Cinda Kornblum, Jennifer Kwon Dobbs & Stefan Liess, Lenfestey Family Foundation, Sarah Lutman & Rob Rudolph, the Carol & Aaron Mack Charitable Fund of the Minneapolis Foundation, George & Olga Mack, Joshua Mack & Ron Warren, Gillian McCain, Mary & Malcolm McDermid, Sjur Midness & Briar Andresen, Maureen Millea Smith & Daniel Smith, Peter Nelson & Jennifer Swenson, Enrique Olivarez, Jr. & Jennifer Komar, Alan Polsky, Marc Porter & James Hennessy, Robin Preble, Alexis Scott, Ruth Stricker Dayton, Jeffrey Sugerman & Sarah Schultz, Nan G. & Stephen C. Swid, Patricia Tilton, Joanne Von Blon, Stu Wilson & Melissa Barker, Warren D. Woessner & Iris C. Freeman, Margaret Wurtele, and Wayne P. Zink & Christopher Schout.

For more information about the Publisher's Circle and other ways to support Coffee House Press books, authors, and activities, please visit www.coffeehousepress.org/support or contact us at info@coffeehousepress.org.

LATIN AMERICAN TRANSLATIONS FROM
COFFEE HOUSE PRESS

Among Strange Victims
Daniel Saldaña París
Translated by Christina MacSweeney

Camanchaca
Diego Zúñiga
Translated by Megan McDowell

Comemadre
Roque Larraquy
Translated by Heather Cleary

Faces in the Crowd
Valeria Luiselli
Translated by Christina MacSweeney

Sidewalks
Valeria Luiselli
Translated by Christina MacSweeney

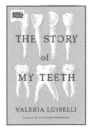

The Story of My Teeth
Valeria Luiselli
Translated by Christina MacSweeney

Empty Set was designed by
Bookmobile Design & Digital Publisher Services.
Text is set in Adobe Caslon Pro.